the girl who learned to live

Ian Lawton

Rational Spirituality Press

First published in 2012 by Rational Spirituality Press.
Second Edition 2022.

All enquiries to be directed to www.rspress.org.

A CIP catalogue record for this title is available from the British Library.

ISBN 978-1-7391445-0-0

Cover design by Ian Lawton.
Cover photograph by Lilkar, licensed by dreamstime.com.
Interior pictures by Ian Lawton.
Author photograph by Miroslawa Kurzydlowska.

one

'And this year's winner of the Orange Prize for women's fiction is...'

The smartly dressed, sassy woman at the lectern pauses for effect. The tension has been building. Various speeches have been made and other, lesser prizes presented over the last hour, but now this is the big one. The expectant energy permeates every corner of the room.

Unusually she hasn't harped on about what a difficult job the panel faced, instead revealing that – with no disrespect to the other finalists – the final choice was an easy and unanimous one.

Finally she breaks the silence.

'The winner is...'

two

All you need is love. Isn't that how the old Beatles classic goes? What they mean is that all you need is to *be loved*. By someone. Anyone. A lover, child, friend – *anyone*.

But is even that really true? When it comes down to it, to be loved is great, fantastic, magical even – but is it *essential*? Surely all we really *need* is to have *someone else need us*. Not in that unhealthy way of a needy partner, that's not what I mean at all. No, we need someone, *anyone*, to need us, in *some* way. They might be a spouse, partner or lover, but they might equally be a child, parent or sibling, or some other family member, or a friend – even a boss or colleague, customer or client. Just someone, *anyone*, who needs us in *some* capacity.

Yes, that's what it comes down to: to survive as a human being, on an emotional level, we need someone to need us in some way. Or, to turn it around, if we're *not* needed in *any way* by *anyone*, our life ceases to have purpose or meaning. We almost cease to exist. It's the darkest place our mind can ever visit. I know. I've been there. Sure, we all have our ups and downs in life. More than that though, there was a time when I lost everything. Yes, *everything*. Work, friends, house, partner... the lot. That's when your belief in yourself and in life itself is tested to the full.

But I also know something else. There's always light at the end of the tunnel. Or, more precisely, you can always *create* that light... *if* you know the secret.

three

I'm pretty sure that the day the acceptance letter came through was the first time I felt genuine pride. It was the summer of 1996 and I'd taken it upstairs to my room to open in private – especially because, as always, I feared the worst. Yet there it was in black and white. I'd actually been accepted by one of the top universities in the country. It was also the first time I ever felt wanted, and the fact it was by an institution not a person did nothing to dampen my joy.

I calmed myself and slowly descended the stairs into the kitchen, holding the precious missive, not wanting to make a fuss but hoping against hope that this, surely *this*, would make him proud and happy too? I sat down on the opposite side of the table and watched him. Squat frame encased in the ubiquitous brown cardigan and grey nylon slacks that made up the entirety of his casual wardrobe, shortish, wavy hair thinning and greying even though he hadn't yet hit forty, his mouth was bulging with fried breakfast in the midst of a face sufficiently reddened that it always looked ready to explode.

'The university has accepted me.'

Even my timid voice seemed to shatter the silence and, clearly taken by surprise, mother looked up from the sink that seemed her almost permanent residence. Aside from the yellow rubber gloves immersed in bubbles she was slim and neat in purple blouse and grey, knee-length skirt, her dark brown hair tied up in a bun. Was it my imagination, or did her eyes momentarily light up? Whatever. Gaze returned to the sink, her mask of indifference was restored so swiftly it was easy to believe it had never slipped. She left any response to father, as always, and he didn't even look up from the paper propped against the teapot.

'That'll be another three years o' draining us bleedin' dry then. 'Ere was me thinkin' you might finally get a proper job an' move out an' all. Now I s'pose you'll be wantin' to stay 'ere, scroungin' off us as per, while I work me bleedin' arse off down the 'ospital?'

I had to turn away so he wouldn't see me fighting back the tears. I didn't want to give him that pleasure. The truth was I'd had a variety of odd jobs ever since I was old enough for a paper round, and done everything I could *not* to be a drain on his low porter's wages. Especially in the last few years I'd worked really hard during school holidays and at weekends, serving in cafes and the like, so I could give mother as much housekeeping as I could afford. That was on top of studying often late into the night to pass my exams, to the extent that I barely knew what a social life was.

Yet even now he couldn't be proud of me. Instead I had to be reminded what an encumbrance I was to them. I must have been crazy to hold out any hope of a different reaction – even more to let it have any effect after all this time. Of course in a sense I *was* crazy, he'd *made* me crazy, but I didn't know that then.

I took a moment to compose myself before turning back. 'I've tried really hard not to be a burden on you both, and I don't want to be one in the future. I've applied for a full grant and, if I carry on working too, I should be able to move out. I realise that would be best for all of us.'

Again mother looked up and seemed about to say something, but once more discretion got the better of her. Yet as our eyes met she allowed a faint but tortured smile to cross her face – enough to suggest she might actually be proud and would miss me after I'd gone, even if she couldn't say it. I smiled back weakly.

Father? He just grunted, and carried on with his breakfast.

Of course she wasn't my real mother, nor he my father, it's just that's what I'd always called them. I must have been around five when she sat me down and told me my real mum was her younger sister, and that when I was very young she'd 'dumped me on them and done a runner'. I had no memories of her at all, but was told never to ask questions about or even mention her. I wasn't allowed to see a photo. I didn't even know her name.

So for as long as I can remember father would tell me, regularly and in no uncertain terms, that I was a useless good-for-nothing who stretched him way beyond his limited means. In other words he wanted me no more than my real mum had – which itself appeared to be not at all. Mother was far less harsh, but so in his thrall that she'd never contradict him by coming to my defence. In fact she never said anything much at all.

I'm not telling you this because I want you to pity me, even though that would be perfectly understandable. It's like a caged animal *born* in captivity: sure it's cruel and unnatural, but it's a lot easier if it's never known anything different. Same with me and rejection. You don't have the same reactions as other people, you're cut off from them. You learn to cut *yourself* off from them.

Probably the closest I got to self-pity was to be envious of the few other kids at school whose parents seemed to love or even spoil them, but there were plenty in much the same boat as me. The only problem was they appeared far more battle-hardened, and rejected me as too soft to be worthy of anything other than contempt. In fact many of them came from completely dysfunctional families where physical abuse, both sexual and otherwise, was rife. Whereas at least my abuse was merely mental. Did that make it easier? Who knows? I certainly don't.

It was also selective, because my parents doted on my immeasurably superior sister. Two years my senior, Kim was everything I wasn't. She was popular and outgoing; I was quiet and introverted. She was athletic, graceful, tall and strong; I was clumsy, awkward, short and skinny. She was beautiful, with long, flowing, blonde locks, clear skin and blue eyes; I was an ugly duckling, my limp, brown hair always cropped short, my thin face blotchy and liberally sprinkled with spots. All I had apparently, even if I struggled to accept it, was a half-decent brain – but that just seemed to make things worse, and she more than anyone loved to make my life a misery. Above all, of course, she was their *real* daughter.

There were, though, a few saving graces in my childhood from which I derived enormous pleasure, which in turn enabled me to survive the rejection.

We lived in a cramped semi on a new-ish council estate in one of the poorer suburbs of southeast London, and with home life as it was I loved to be outside whenever possible. For as long as I can remember my parents didn't seem to care if I was unsupervised, and there was a small park nearby – it was just a patch of grass really, with a few struggling bushes and a small kid's playground – but it was *outdoors*, and that meant everything. No one to shout at me, maybe the odd bird to sing with or squirrel to talk to, feeling the sun or rain or wind on my face and not much minding which – they all made me feel fresh and *alive*.

Better still if I had more time, and especially if there were other kids in the park itching to taunt the misfit, I'd just *run* – and I seemed to be able to go for miles without getting tired. I guess if I'd been able to demonstrate this one athletic talent at school I might have been more popular, but our sports curriculum didn't stretch to cross country. Anyway I didn't really like competition, and it was the solitude that appealed. So I'd just run and run for miles, wherever the fancy took me.

My favourite destination was the park at Greenwich, where I'd push myself in a final spurt up the hill to the famous observatory. As I caught my breath I'd stare out across the wide expanse of lush grass dotted with trees that flowed down to the classical facades of the Naval College below, with the river beyond. This, to me, was heaven. I'd stand there for hours, musing on the lives of those who'd fashioned this wonderful vista, or had lived or strolled here in the intervening centuries. Occasionally I'd wonder why I couldn't have a life of privilege and luxury like that, but usually I'd stop myself before long. Why ruin such wonderful moments by being sad?

I had a favourite tree too, that I'd sit beneath to read. With no satellite TV, computer games, internet or social media, books were the easiest escape for someone as socially inept as me – and I was an avid reader, withdrawing as many as I could from the library every week. I was soon drawn to the classic novels because of the way they conjured up times past: Austen, Hardy, Dickens, that sort of thing. Then as time went on I'd read anything I could lay my hands on: fiction, non-fiction, art, science, history – literally anything that caught my attention. I guess that's what gave me a head start at school, even if being seen as a nerdy swot hardly enhanced my popularity. It's also why, when the time came, they encouraged me to seek a place at university, because without their prompting I'd have had far too little self-belief.

Although I loved solitude, I can even remember one *family* event that wasn't entirely painful. We rarely went on holiday, although when father finally had a decent win on the football pools he really splashed out, whisking mother and Kim off to sunny Spain for a week. Of course he said he couldn't afford to take me too, so I was packed off to distant relatives – which was actually a nice break for me because, while not exactly friendly, at least they pretty much ignored me and didn't rant the whole time.

In any case I was around fourteen when we took the holiday *I* most remember. Needless to say he made a huge song and dance about the expense of taking us *all* down to the evocatively named 'Isle of Purbeck' in Dorset, but I refused to let that dampen my excitement at such an adventure. After riding since early morning in various coaches and buses, in the evening we finally reached our destination: a campsite in a small village on the outskirts of the seaside town of Swanage.

I instantly fell in love with the whole place. We'd taken the train out east on day trips to Southend a few times, which made a nice change, but strictly speaking it was only in the mouth of the Thames. By contrast this felt like *real* sea, and *real* countryside!

The town itself was quaint. Clustered around the southern end of a picturesque bay, its main streets were lined with the usual mix of tourist and chip shops, arcades, ice cream kiosks, cafes, pubs and so on. But then there was the beach, with sand not stones! For the first time ever I could run in the gentle surf, letting the water splash up my legs and body, then stopping to squelch the soggy mixture between my toes. This was an entirely new version of heaven!

I just wished it could've been less busy. That summer was seriously hot and the place seemed to be packed with noisy, sweaty, bright-pink visitors trying to control their wayward children, while indulging their favourite pastime of queuing for anything and everything. I didn't pretend to understand their motives for coming away at all, it didn't seem much of a rest – but then I realised that my family were pretty much the same. So I just blanked them all out and daydreamed about what it would be like out-of-season.

My parents weren't great walkers, but the doctor had

told father he needed more exercise, so I begged them to let us all go for a picnic up on the Purbeck Ridge that rose majestically from the edge of our campsite. But my pleas fell on deaf ears, until the day when even Kim couldn't resist the lure of a clear blue sky and decided it was a good idea after all – at which point they of course relented. But this was no time to let a little family politics ruin my excitement!

I got to the top long before the others, leaving their general complaints about walking up hills in such heat far behind. I even got to run around on the Ridge for a while as they busied themselves with the tartan blanket, sausage rolls, lemonade and suchlike that were now the subjects of their entire focus. Spread out in front of me was a long, gently undulating plateau of wiry grass interspersed with thorn bushes. Running over to the far side it fell away down a wooded slope and, using a map from the campsite, I could see that several miles of scrubby heath separated us from the broad vista of Poole Harbour to the north. Beyond its narrow entrance lay the exclusive Sandbanks, with the long golden sands of Bournemouth beach curving far into the distance.

Further along the Ridge to the west a cluster of tumuli dominated the landscape. I'd never actually seen one before, only read about them being constructed back in the mists of time to revere long-dead chiefs and warriors, so I ran to the top of the largest at double speed to drink in the energy and admire the equally spectacular southern view. Beneath me lay a broad, green valley in which a narrow ribbon of road wound its way through the hamlets and farmsteads lying between Swanage to my left and the ancient ruins of Corfe Castle, which could just be seen perched on its own, smaller hill several miles up to my right. On the far side the valley rose gently to a parallel, more southerly ridge, beyond which lay the sea. I wished I could sit there forever, but sadly time was moving on and I needed to return to the others.

But, as if all that wasn't enough, on the way back I was startled by a loud whistle. Following its direction I spotted small clouds of virgin white steam billowing from a coppice down in the valley and, while I couldn't see clearly without binoculars, I knew it had to be the local steam train! I'd read about this before we came down, as well as having devoured *The Railway Children* several times some years before, and this real-life reminder of a gentler, bygone era left me absolutely spellbound. Perhaps for the first time in my life I experienced complete and utter bliss and just basked in the moment, my grin so wide my jaw actually started to ache.

When I rejoined the others for the walk back down it was apparent they'd paid minimal heed to the views or the train, having taken their lead from father. He was, as usual, preoccupied with moaning about anything and everything, and wasn't going to let a wonderful, new environment change the habits of a lifetime.

Nevertheless later in the week, when we were in the town, I was determined to visit the train station while the others sat on the beach. It was utterly charming, with a proper period ticket office, genuine signs and porters' trolleys on the platforms, and even better a café housed in an authentic dining carriage. I had just enough for a glass of lemonade and a sticky bun, and I sat at a small table at the far end from the serving counter, watching the visitors come and go.

Aided by the musty smell of old cloth upholstery, and by wood polished to a high sheen by the countless touches of unknown predecessors, I escaped – not unusual for me, as you already know – into a world in which they were all in period costume being incredibly polite to each other. Not only did this help to block out the reality of angry parents scolding their ill-behaved offspring, but I even conjured up an image of a dashing young man wooing me at this very table. But then I remembered that such things didn't happen to useless, plain girls like me, and I had to work very hard not to let that ruin the moment.

The timetable showed the train ran regularly, but sadly this wasn't deemed a good use of our limited funds. I was heartbroken but dared not show it, and consoled myself that I'd visited a wonderful place that was completely different from where I lived. One that made a lasting impression on me as – yes, no doubt about it – a whole new slice of heaven.

I also made myself a solemn promise. One day, one way or another, I'd return to ride on that train.

four

The dreams started in the week leading up to my twenty-fifth birthday. They weren't the sort of ordinary dreams that everyone has – you know, the sort where you're walking along and a school friend whose name you can't even remember jumps out and starts talking about something that's been in the news, but before you can respond you suddenly find yourself in a compromising situation with a friend's partner making entirely inappropriate advances and enjoying it way more than you should. That's just your brain's way of processing the trivial information it's picked up recently, mixed in with some genuine screwed up stuff that must be lurking in there too.

No, these were *lucid* ones that seemed incredibly real, and weren't all jumbled up and nonsensical. That might sound wonderful and interesting, and I'm sure some people's lucid dreams are exactly that. But even when mine started off ok they ended up being seriously disturbing, much more like nightmares. They really shocked me.

Even an amateur psychologist might think that was to be expected after everything I'd been through, but it wasn't that simple. You see my life had improved immeasurably after I started college in London. Living in various student halls, for the first time ever I wasn't being constantly bullied. I no longer had my family to contend with – it won't surprise you that my trips back home were sporadic at best – and at last I found that being reasonably intelligent wasn't seen as a crime by my fellow students. I lived in a hall of residence not far from the main campus and we'd sit up late into the night discussing everything – our studies, great literature, politics, world affairs, relationships, love – you name it, we discussed it, often with raised voices and strong opinions. This was yet another new slice of heaven for me.

This was just before the advent of tuition fees so plenty of students were mainly there for the drinking and socialising, but I managed to fit into a small group who were intelligent and keen to learn and we really gelled. We were diverse too, in our backgrounds and in what we studied. On top of that, for me reading English Lit was a real pleasure – a bit like being paid to do what you enjoy anyway. But this also meant that for the first time I understood that time really *does* fly when you're having fun, because in what seemed like the blink of an eye it was nearly over and I was facing the choice of what to do next.

I'd been through something of a personal transformation too. Whereas I'd spent my adolescence expecting nothing more than a life of lonely banality, perhaps working in a library with books as my only solace, college life had given me some ambition and faith in myself. The shy, awkward adolescent had started to blossom. Apparently I'd even begun to be regarded as attractive. I guess you'd say I was an *acquired taste*, and I was nowhere near as free with my sexual favours as some of my friends. But I was finally exploring the world of relationships first-hand instead of just dreaming or talking about them, even if tentatively at first. Sure there was still room for improvement, but my self-confidence was steadily growing.

I'd worked hard too and, as expected by my tutors although still not fully by me, was on course for a first going into the final year. Meaning that as long as I kept up the good work I pretty much had my pick of careers. This was the mid-nineties, the economy had recovered from the recession at the beginning of the decade and graduate jobs were plentiful. So, what to do?

I remember the conversation with my careers adviser as if it were yesterday, simply because I really didn't have a clue what path I wanted to follow and needed serious help. It felt important, and Sarah – mid-thirties, red trouser suit, slightly over-the-top makeup, blonde bob – seemed to be a worldly, well-informed type.

'Well Zoe, with your predicted grades I'm confident you can go in any direction you like. Any ideas?' She leaned in expectantly across the desk.

'Not really, I'm afraid.' I felt embarrassed and clueless, but she soon set my mind at ease.

'Don't worry... you're in the majority. Not many people have a childhood dream and their future all mapped out. Shall we do some elimination?'

'Sure, good plan.' At least I probably had some idea of what I *didn't* want to do.

'What about continued study? With your grades you could easily do a PhD or Masters. Or maybe you'd prefer to be a tutor, do some lecturing?'

'I don't think so.' I reflected on the years I'd spent with nothing as a child and, although with a full grant college life had been more comfortable, I'd still had to work hard in the holidays to make ends meet across each year. So now the opportunity was there I had a taste for earning some proper money – and, let's not hide the truth, for showing a certain person that I wasn't a useless, sponging good-for-nothing after all. 'No, I'm keen to start earning properly. A high-flying career with a serious salary is definitely the direction I'd like to take.'

'Ok, good, that narrows it down. What about the media? Lots of people do media studies, but a proper first in English would put you well ahead.'

'No... again, I don't think so.' I knew some media types were really talented, but all I could picture was a bunch of two-faced luvvies being paid to have endless pointless meetings and stab each other in the back. It didn't appeal.

'Journalism?'

'Possible.' I thought for a moment. 'No, too cutthroat for me I think.'

'The public sector?'

'Sorry, but that's another no.' I was pretty sure some people in government departments and council offices must be working extremely hard and doing their best against all the odds but, again, all my mind could conjure was images of people making work for themselves, playing office politics and serving out time waiting to qualify for generous pensions.

'Ok, no problem.' She was obviously used to being patient. 'Looks like it's one of the commercial professions for you then.'

I nodded. We were definitely narrowing things down.

'Let's run through them then. Accountancy?'

'Hmm... too much further study, plus it doesn't feel creative enough.'

'Insurance?'

'No... same applies.'

'Banking?'

I paused. This was the first time I hadn't felt an instant aversion, despite having no previous thoughts in this direction. I'd read all about the high flyers who were making more money than they could extravagantly spend and, if they were bright, making it fast. Could *this* be the best way to stick two fingers up to my family in the shortest possible time?

'Tell me more,' I said, to Sarah's evident relief.

To my delight one of the big City firms showed a keen interest, and an impressive starting salary as a trainee trader that would quickly escalate with success. I accepted their offer.

When the time came they were as good as their word. I worked hard to achieve everything expected of me and then some, and within a short time was, indeed, flying high. Suffice to say that soon my salary and bonus combined ran into six figures. Mind you, after all those years of poverty I spent plenty too. I rented a beautiful flat overlooking the Thames, took foreign holidays and indulged in all the luxuries I'd never enjoyed before. I felt I deserved it.

It wasn't too long, though, before I realised I should plan more for the future – and invest in good old bricks and mortar, preferably within easy cycling distance of work. When I collected the keys to a modern, three-bedroom, penthouse flat in one of the new docklands developments I was immensely proud. It wasn't cheap, yet I didn't even need a mortgage.

The one thing I still didn't have in abundance was love – of the romantic kind, anyway. I'd had several relatively short relationships with boyfriends who seemed to love me more than enough – a new and in some ways exciting experience that improved on anything at college. But somehow I knew *I* was holding something back. Nevertheless I contented myself with the thought that I just hadn't met *the one*, and there was plenty of time.

In any case I had a good circle of friends by this time too, colleagues I got on ok with and those from college I still saw. True there was still no really special companion, no one that I felt saw life through exactly the same lens as me, but again I didn't let that worry me too much.

The big surprise was that I started to get on with Kim for the first time. We'd had little contact since I left home – all I knew was that she was still living nearby in a shared flat and working in a local beauty salon – but when she heard I was in the money she got back in touch. I guess I'd always known she was pretty materialistic, but I didn't mind. It was cathartic for me that she was almost looking up to me now. She came to stay on a regular basis and we grew close in a strange kind of way.

'You *must* have some real dishy friends darlin', when you gonna let Kimmy meet 'em?' came the regular refrain. Although still somewhat high-pitched her voice wasn't *too* annoying, albeit she'd retained the vernacular of our youth that I'd deliberately shed long before.

I tried to put her off gently: 'Kim, sweetheart, I'm not sure any of them would really be your *type*?'

'Oh come on Zo, just give us a *chance* will you? I'm like a friggin' cock magnet, me!' Although she didn't quite have father's aptitude for bad language, she could nevertheless be quite bawdy when the mood took her.

I doubt you will be for these boys I thought. Still I eventually relented. Several times. Each one a disaster. Unlike the lads she knew at school and near home, my male friends tended to look beyond her obvious good looks. Bless her, now she'd stepped out from father's shadow she'd become a much nicer person than the vindictive, self-centred cow I'd had to live with. But she was just out of her depth and not on their wavelength at all. She wasn't really on mine, yet I guess our shared background was enough.

One day when I was feeling particularly adventurous I tried to broach the subject of how she and our parents had made me feel when I was younger. 'Kimmy, you know I wasn't treated very well when we were kids, don't you?'

'I dunno what you're on about doll. Dad was bleedin' hard on us both.'

'I don't think that's quite fair Kim. He worshipped the ground you walked on, whereas I... well let's just say he didn't have a lot of time for me.'

'No idea where you're gettin' that from love.' She looked genuinely bemused. 'Like I said, far as I remember we was treated the same.'

Was I going mad? Had I imagined it all? No... of course I hadn't! But somehow she'd persuaded herself this was the truth and was in complete denial. There was clearly no point in pursuing the matter or trying to make a big point, when anything I said would just fall on deaf ears. So I learned to let it ride, and just enjoy our reversal of roles.

Things still ran very deep with father though, and there was little thawing. I was sending mother a tidy sum of money every month – feeling it my duty, whatever had happened between us – and in our occasional, brief calls and visits she seemed to be reasonably grateful. But he refused to show any sort of softening or appreciation, continuing to see anything I gave them as his right, even though I was more than generous. He really was a bitter man. If he'd refused my money out of pride I'd have had more respect for him, but he didn't.

I didn't care though. I'd done what I set out to do and stuck two fingers up at him. *Who's the waste of space now?*

All things considered, then, life was good. Really good. I was enjoying myself, perhaps even more than at college, especially now I had money too.

You might have thought, and I'd have had to agree with you, that I deserved some happiness after everything I'd overcome. But someone or something had other plans... and mine was about to be rudely disrupted.

five

The boy must be about four or five. He's wearing simple, country clothes, clean enough but well worn, his straight dark hair matches his brooding eyes, and he has a serious air. What appears to be his brother is sitting next to him, forming a complete contrast. With tousled fair hair and piercing blue eyes, he's laughing and joking with the other children around him.

They're sitting at the back of a simple, one-room schoolhouse, with a blackboard at the front and various pictures and notices on the walls. Each child sits at a small, wooden desk, while a larger one faces them at the front. A wide, low bookcase in the front-left corner, opposite the door, holds a motley assortment of well-thumbed books.

The scene changes when a girl of similar age walks in, her blonde hair falling in ringlets over her shoulders. The boy jolts upright in his chair, almost as if he's been struck by lightning. He stares open-mouthed as she's ushered to a desk near the front by the teacher who has followed her in. His brother turns briefly to inspect the new arrival but seems disinterested, soon returning his attention to his friends.

The teacher calls for order and brings the girl out to the front to introduce herself. Though understandably shy, to the boy the smile she casts around the room has an entrancing radiance that perfectly matches the warmth in her twinkling green eyes.

There's no doubt about it.

He may be young, but he's smitten. Totally, utterly, completely, irreversibly smitten.

The boy, his brother and the girl are running along the edge of a field of ripe corn, laughing and shouting as they go. Older now, perhaps in their early teens, they're clearly close friends. Under a deep blue sky they climb over a gate and run on, down a grassy embankment dotted with trees to a river at the bottom.

The boys quickly strip down to their underclothes and dive in, laughing and splashing each other. The girl watches intently, looking from one to the other, almost as if making a difficult choice, but they remain oblivious.

Soon though she's forced to answer their calls to join them or suffer the penalty of being thrown in fully clothed. She slips off her sandals and simple, white, summer dress and dives in gracefully. She stays underwater for some time before surfacing right in front of the boy's brother and, throwing her arms round his shoulders, planting a kiss firmly on his lips. It lasts for several seconds before she pushes him away and swims off, laughing, as if nothing has happened. Momentarily stunned, he recovers and splashes off after her.

The boy quietly slips out of the water. For several minutes he sits motionless a little way up the slope, head down, arms wrapped around his drawn-up legs, unnoticed by the others still frolicking in the water.

Suddenly he stands up, grabs his clothes and runs at full pelt back up the hill.

Now in their late teens, the boy and girl are on horseback on another wonderful summer's day. They ride along side by side, comfortable in their silence. His brother is nowhere to be seen.

They make their way along the edge of the same field as before and on down to the river. They dismount under the shade of a clump of trees and the girl spreads a simple blanket on the ground. The boy helps her unpack the picnic she's prepared, but when she offers him a large chunk of bread and some cheese he politely refuses. As she eats he lies back on the ground looking up through the branches at the cloudless blue sky.

When she's finished her food she lies back too, resting her head on his lap, body at right angles. There's still little conversation but the boy seems increasingly restless. He suddenly sits up, forcing her to do likewise, and is clearly about to say something when a neighbour comes into view, strolling along the riverbank. They nod in acknowledgment and then, when he's finally passed by, she turns back – only to be met with silence and a far-off gaze. She asks what's wrong but he gets up and saunters down to the river, head bowed. She runs after him and around to his front, grabbing him firmly by the shoulders and staring up into his tortured face, pleading with him to tell her what's the matter. He looks away. His lips do not move.

Slowly the girl lets him go and turns back, defeated. She packs up the food in silence and rides off alone. The boy remains motionless, staring into the depths of the river.

The large wooden hut is festooned with flowers and other decorations, the tables littered with food and drink, the scene one of obvious merriment. Everyone holds hands to form a circle, the assorted musicians strike up a high tempo and they all begin to dance around the boy's brother and the girl. They gaze raptly into each other's eyes as he swings her around and around, skirt rising as she twirls to reveal fine, shapely legs. It becomes clear that it's a wedding party and the whole village is attending.

Yet one figure sits alone outside the circle. The boy is now a man in his early twenties. Slouched over a corner table his head rests on folded arms, empty bottles strewn liberally around.

When the dance is over a fine-looking, dark-haired girl rushes over to rouse him. She points to where a new dance has begun and he rises unsteadily to his feet but then, roughly pushing her aside, staggers off to the door. She looks longingly after him but doesn't try to follow.

The boy is now a man of around forty, his long, unkempt, greying hair matching his beard. His small wooden hut has no decorations and the furniture is decrepit and sparse. His clothing matches his surroundings.

His one concession to comfort seems to be an old rocking chair in which he sits alone, gently swaying back and forth, back and forth. His face is blank and his eyes lifeless as he stares through the window at the fields of corn.

Six

That first set of dreams in mid 2003 followed a pattern that was to be repeated several times over the next few years. Each set involved separate dreams on consecutive nights, with each one revealing a different scene that seemed to pick up coherently from where the previous one left off.

I told you they got progressively worse, and that last one really spooked me. By the end I wasn't just *watching* the man as he sat alone in his chair day after day, mourning the love he'd refused to openly admit in order to make way for the brother he also loved. No. By the end I *was* him. I was *seeing* through his eyes, *feeling* his intense pain.

This was the trigger for the emergence of a sense of unease that somehow all was *not* as it seemed – in terms of both life in general and my life in particular. What's more fuel was only added to the fire when the messages then started to appear.

One Saturday morning early the following year I was taking a bath. Kim was staying over for the weekend and I'd just had a hard week at work so we planned a lazy one. I was relaxing and taking my time. But when I emerged and stood in front of the mirror I was confronted by a hand-written message that had only become visible when highlighted by the steam:

who are you?

'Ha, ha, ha... very funny,' I called out to her.

'What you on about?' came her sleepy voice from the

spare bedroom.

'You know perfectly well. The message on the mirror.' I had to admit this really wasn't Kim's style, but I knew the flat was secure and I'd had no other visitors all week, so it had to have been her. There was a lengthy delay as she dragged herself out of bed and appeared in the doorway scratching at her tousled hair. I hardly even felt the usual guilty pleasure that she too could look pretty disastrous when she'd just woken up, especially now she was approaching her late twenties.

'I dunno *what* you're talkin' about,' she mumbled just before she saw the mirror. '*I* never wrote that!' She seemed pretty adamant.

'Well *I* didn't, so it *must* have been you.'

'I'm friggin' tellin' you I *never*!' Now she was *really* adamant, and I didn't want a full-blown row.

'Ok, ok, I'm sorry. I thought you were trying to play some sort of joke on me, but obviously not.'

'*Thank you*. S'not even funny anyway.' She was about to walk off when she turned back, smiling down at me: 'To make up for it you can bring us brekky in bed.'

'Of course, whatever madam desires.' I smiled back as I gave her a hug, but when she'd gone I looked again at the message. She must have written it in her sleep or something, although even then it seemed pretty screwed up. But with no other explanation to hand I just had to let it go. Those first dreams were still pretty vivid, I didn't need this freaking me out too.

This uneasy truce with myself was shattered only a few weeks later. The same thing happened, again on a Saturday morning after a bath, but this time Kim was nowhere to be seen:

are you happy?

This was now officially weirding me out. *Who am I?* Just little old me! *Am I happy?* Yes! Apart from the dreams and these messages, I'm very happy for once, thank you very much!

I tried to forget about them and just get on with my life. But whoever was behind the messages clearly didn't want that because, just in case I needed any further confirmation it wasn't Kim, a third appeared on the mirror after a similar interval when I was again alone:

who do you love?

That clinched it. However weird it was, someone, or some *thing*, was either trying to send me mad or really wanted me to think about these questions. I considered these two options over a strong cup of coffee, and decided it was best to assume the latter – unless or until I had some proof to the contrary. What's more it was clear there was really only one place to properly consider them.

Incredibly I hadn't visited my old haunt at Greenwich Park since I left home. As a student it had been some way off, so I guess over time my memories had faded. But now they came flooding back, bringing genuine excitement at the prospect of returning. Not only that but it was the same sort of distance as when I'd been at home, and I could run there again. That felt right, although I hadn't run at all for ages. You know how easy it is, when you *grow up* and become preoccupied with work and adult life, to forget the simple pleasures that once made you happy as a child.

I needn't have worried. I had to stop a few times to catch my breath but it was wonderful to find I hadn't lost it completely. In fact running again really cleared my head and I didn't think about the messages at all till I got to the park – where, after immersing myself in the view from the observatory for a while, I ran back down to my favourite old tree and sat beneath it.

So, to the first question: who are you? Try as I might I struggled to get anywhere with this one. Short of asking *why are you here?* it was about as existential as you could get. I reflected on how I'd gone through a phase of studying all the great religious texts of the world – and on how some passages, especially in those with a more eastern flavour, had really resonated with what I knew to be my intuitive, right brain. Then at college, when conversations with science-oriented friends had brought my left-brained, analytical head more to the fore, I'd been drawn to study the work of existential philosophers like Nietzsche, Heidegger and Sartre.

But increasingly since I'd started work I'd hardly thought about such things at all. I was seeing less and less of my old college pals, and these just weren't the sort of topics my new friends and colleagues discussed. Actually I'd soon have become a pariah again if I'd even admitted to thinking about them in the go-getting, materialistic environment I now inhabited. If anyone ever did bring up the subject of religion, which was extremely rare, I now classified myself as at best agnostic, possibly downright atheist.

Ok, let's leave that one and move on to the next question: are you happy? I'd dismissed this with a simple *yes* a few weeks earlier, but now it was clearly time to think more deeply. Compared to how I'd felt all the time I'd been living with my parents, that superficial answer was a no-brainer. What's more I'd been so relieved to at last have a life with some status, recognition, friends and money that I'd been happy to leave it at that. All perfectly understandable, don't you think? And yet... now I was being forced to seriously consider the question, by the very act of opening it up for genuine debate my intuition had instantly produced the true answer. *No, I'm not. Not really. Not deep down where it matters.*

It was now I realised that my musings about the first question had opened a real can of worms. I'd been so caught up in my new life that I'd happily glossed over any problems. But the real truth was that now the only things I discussed with my friends and colleagues was how much money we were making, how easy it was and what we'd spend it all on. So in not being able to talk about things metaphysical and philosophical, or indeed anything of genuine importance, I was cutting off a hugely important part of myself. Nor had I allowed it to find expression in any other outlet, with other friends or further study or whatever. I'd just shut that side of myself down, and in that instant I knew I could no longer.

So what about the third question: who do you love? This was perhaps the strangest one of all. I've already admitted that I still hadn't allowed myself to become properly close to any boyfriend, or any other friend for that matter. So now I had to think hard. Could I keep writing this off as the result of not having met the right one and so on? Again *no*. Now I really considered it I felt there must have been a reason why I'd been holding myself back.

As I sat and pondered further it came to me that I needed to turn the question inwards. *Do you love yourself?* Of course I knew that lots of gurus and self-help books maintain this is really important, but until now I'd written it off with the lazy answer. *Of course I do! Look at where I am now compared to where I came from. I'm PROUD of myself!* Yet now I was being forced to really think the true answer was again all too clear. I wasn't really being me. I'd sold out. Quite understandably maybe, but I'd sold out all the same, and I wasn't truly at peace with that.

That's how it dawned on me that, just as the timid, bullied, adolescent me didn't represent the *true* Zoe, nor did the more confident but materialistic adult me. It was time to find out for the first time who I really was, and to learn to fully accept and love her. Only then would I be able to give myself properly to someone else.

But now an even more daunting question raised its head. How would I go about it?

Seven

When I finally got to ride on the steam train at Swanage it turned out to be a far more pivotal moment in my life than I might have expected.

This was another memory from my childhood that had somewhat faded. It seems I'd even blocked off the pleasant times as all related to a period of my life I'd rather forget. But even as I sat under the tree in the park one thing became crystal clear about my journey to get to know myself properly. It had to begin with a week away from work and from London, and not on a beach or skiing holiday as was now my norm. Almost immediately my time in the Dorset countryside flashed into my head – and what could possibly fit the bill better than a retreat to revisit that happy time and give myself space to think? I'd climb up onto the Purbeck Ridge with the wonderful views, and best of all I'd fulfil the promise I'd made all those years ago and take that train ride.

One thing I didn't need to revisit, though, was a tent on a campsite. I'd become somewhat used to luxury now, so when I got home I found what appeared to be one of the best hotels in the town and, to my great delight, it was no problem to book what was described as a *superior* double room for the first week in March – well before the holiday season started. That was two weeks away, which would give me enough time to organise things at work.

I travelled down at a leisurely pace on the Sunday – on

the assumption that public transport would be less crowded – taking the train from Waterloo to Wareham before switching to a bus for the final leg of the journey. I could easily have afforded a taxi, but I wanted to arrive by the same route I had as a child. The town looked as quaint as ever, lots of memories came flooding back both good and bad, and in real life the hotel was every bit as imposing and

luxurious as its pictures. Located halfway up the narrow high street that winds its way up from the sea, it had been constructed by George Burt – dubbed the 'King of Swanage' because he'd overseen the development of much of the town in the late Victorian era. According to the guidebooks, for what was then his personal residence he had adopted the 'Scottish Baronial style' to imitate a feudal castle.

After settling in to my luxurious four-postered room I enjoyed a fine dinner in the wood-panelled restaurant before locating the bar to indulge myself with a nightcap. Surprisingly for such a cosy and well-appointed room it was empty apart from the smartly dressed barman. However it soon became clear this was perhaps down to his mixing obsequiousness with clumsy flirting, which rather ruined the experience and soon forced me to retire. I did however glean that the steam train only ran at weekends in the off-season, which meant the highlight of my trip would have to be put off till the following Saturday. On a more positive note, in the years since my earlier visit the service had been extended from a short trip just out of the town to one that followed the valley right through to Corfe Castle and even a little beyond, which would make for a proper ride.

This gave me the idea that I'd like a better view of the edifice from which said village derives its name than the obscured version I'd had in the twilight on the bus. So the following morning I jogged out to the campsite on the outskirts where we'd stayed all those years before, retraced the climb up onto the Ridge, and ran along to the tumuli, stopping to catch my breath and admire the views. But then I carried on for several miles until I had a proper view of a structure that, for all its ruined incompleteness, was still somehow proud and defiant.

Spread out on a small hill in the valley below, the castle had a hugely atmospheric, Gothic feel, even though it was originally erected in Norman times. I had read that, having been twice besieged as a Royalist stronghold during the Civil War of the seventeenth century, its final surrender led to much of its imposing structure being deliberately blown to smithereens. But enough remains for it to be quite breathtakingly beautiful, especially in its magnificent surroundings – not least the small, picturesque village itself that nestles underneath its protective wing, all the buildings constructed using local Purbeck stone.

With Tuesday and Thursday set aside for relaxing in the hotel and town, on the Wednesday I again jogged out to the edge to climb up onto the Ridge. But this time I took the right-hand path in the cleft where the road runs through, signposted to the mysterious sounding 'Old Harry's Rocks'. It was a much steeper ascent than before, but again it levelled out at the top into a broad plateau stretching for some miles. The right-hand side culminated in steep cliffs forming the northern perimeter of Swanage Bay, with stunning views across to the town itself. But continuing on to the northeast it dropped down a gentle slope bounded by steep cliffs.

At their end I could finally see my destination: several vertical chalk stacks that had been separated from the headland by thousands of years of erosion, forming a majestic chain heading out to sea. I'd always suffered from a fear of heights, but I couldn't resist trying to test myself by walking to the edge of the cliffs where, somewhat surprisingly in an increasingly risk averse world, no safety chains or fences were in place to protect the unwary from a vertical drop into the crashing waves over a hundred feet below. Some chance! I ended up crawling on my belly the last few yards and, even then, just popping my head up to peer even the tiniest bit over the edge induced severe nausea and an anxious retreat to safety. I could only marvel at the calm of the people who casually walked right up and looked over as if it were nothing at all.

On the Friday I went in the other direction completely, out through Durlston Country Park to the south of the town and along the coastal path heading west. At one point it dropped down to a quarry used as a defence station during the war, where extensive caves had been tunnelled back into the base of the cliff, with huge pillars left in place here and there to support the vast expanse of flat roof. From there it was on to St Aldhelm's Head, some five miles from the town, with its tiny ancient chapel and coastal lookout station backed by a row of remote, windswept cottages accessible only by a long, narrow track. The views out across the sea and further along the coast were magnificent.

I had still seen very little of the British countryside outside London, but there was no doubt... this Jurassic Coast really was a special place.

In any case, all of this was just a prelude to the train! On the Friday evening as I drifted off to sleep I drew on the long-buried memories of hearing the whistle and seeing the plume of smoke all those years before. As I closed my eyes I *was* that wide-eyed little girl back on the Ridge again. The trouble was – I know it seems childish – but my excitement was so great I woke up in the middle of the night and couldn't get back to sleep. This was quite rare for me, although eventually I did manage to nod off again.

When I drew back the curtains it was a fine, clear morning. I opened the window and tested the air. Fantastic! It was a much warmer day, indeed remarkably warm for the time of year and, just as I'd hoped, I'd be able to wear the classic, white cotton dress I'd brought specially to transport myself back to that bygone era. Deciding to skip breakfast, in no time I was wrapping a cardigan round my shoulders and donning the wide-brimmed, straw hat that was a big favourite but hadn't had an outing since the previous summer. I checked in the mirror as I was leaving. *Not bad today Zo… not bad at all.*

I made my way to the town centre, attracting rather more stealthy, admiring glances from the few men I passed en route than I'd normally expect, which made me more than usually aware of their partners' silent resentment. It forced me to reflect on the double-edged sword of looking great all the time – like Kim, at least once her hair is done and she's put her face on – and made me appreciate the fact I only attracted that kind of attention occasionally. Still, I have to admit it only added to my general gaiety and sense of wellbeing.

The station was just as charming as ever, and the timetable revealed that the sole train operating hadn't long departed, and wouldn't be back and ready to leave again for some time. With time to kill I bought a ticket and repaired to the café in the old dining carriage, feeling that a cup of coffee and a bite to eat wouldn't do me any harm. This too was much as I remembered it, the general ambience and smell unchanged, except it was nowhere near as busy in the off-season.

I was at the till and just about to pay when a soft, well-spoken voice in my ear brought me up short.

'Perhaps you would do me the honour of allowing me to buy your breakfast?' I turned to find the most beautiful hazel eyes I'd ever seen staring evenly into mine.

Shit! Sorry, I don't normally swear, but this called for it. I'd been chatted up plenty of times before, but I'd never been put on the spot quite like this. I was torn. One part of me was screaming *Just accept!* no questions asked. But another clearly felt that just wouldn't be good form, and was resisting. Yet he was so polite, and what he'd said was so in keeping with the manners of the bygone era I'd come to recapture that surely it would be churlish to refuse? Especially given that he was bloody gorgeous as well! In fact he seemed to be acting out for real the scenes my imagination had conjured in this very place so long ago.

After what felt like an age of clumsy indecision I came up with what I hoped was a response befitting this momentary time warp.

'Do you normally approach vulnerable young women in such a confident manner, Mr...?'

'Sheridan. Zak Sheridan. No, I most certainly do not. But I'm afraid I saw you walking in with that amazing hat on, and something inside me just kicked in... I had to come and speak to you. I sincerely hope I haven't caused offence, but if I have of course I'll take my leave.'

He was *so* polite, *so* respectful, *so* sweet, and those eyes were still burning into my skull. What could I do? What could *any* girl do except spend however long it would take just waiting for him to sweep her off her feet and declare his undying love? At least that's how *I* felt. After a few misguided attempts to prove how liberated I was at college, I'd come to realise I was something of a traditionalist where romance was concerned. Before I responded I tried to calm myself, and a heart that seemed intent on announcing its stimulation to the whole world by jumping right through the thin fabric of my dress.

'Now you put it like that I can hardly refuse, kind sir. Zoe Smith.' I stretched out my hand and he took it gently in his. Can you believe he actually raised it and gently kissed the back of his own thumb? Wow, when it came to being a proper gentleman this boy really knew his stuff! He lingered just long enough for me to savour the moment before raising his head. His eyes hadn't left mine the whole time.

'I'm delighted to make your acquaintance Miss Smith.' I returned his broad smile with a more restrained version of my own, both of us clearly delighting in playing up to our period roles. 'Now isn't it fascinating that we both have the same initials? Surely dear lady fate has brought us together for some higher purpose?'

'Well sir, I must allow that it *is* rather a coincidence.' I tried to keep a straight face, but we realised simultaneously that we'd taken the play-acting far enough and started to giggle. Yet we continued to stare into each other's eyes, and I could feel myself melting. It's clichéd I know, but it really did seem as if I'd known him forever. Our reverie was finally interrupted by a cough from the plump, middle-aged woman in a blue apron behind the counter, who had apparently stopped everything she'd been doing, her stare now alternating between the two of us, mouth slightly ajar.

'Don't mind me my lovelies.' She was shaking her head as she smiled. 'It's not every day you get to see a proper love story like in the films acted out right in front of your very eyes! You sure there's not a camera hiding somewhere?'

'Sorry,' we said in unison, suddenly reminded that there was still a world revolving around us.

'May I?' I nodded and Zak took my tray, carefully transferring its contents to his own. 'Perhaps you'd like to pick a table while I sort this out?' He was such a gentleman, even now we were no longer role-playing.

'Sure, thank you.' With few other customers it will come as no surprise that I made my way to the very table at the far end where I'd sat and daydreamed as a girl. Good lord! Was I just about to make them a reality?

Said table also afforded me time to get a good view of Zak before he came to join me. Not especially tall, in fact probably only a few inches taller than me, his tight white shirt and close-fitting blue jeans nevertheless showed he was slim and lithe. He looked fit, like he worked out. Apart from his entrancing eyes he had well-defined cheeks and a strong jaw line, yet his smooth-shaven face was still boyish, surmounted by shoulder-length, curly, light-brown hair that looked as though it would be wonderfully soft to the touch. He exuded fun and confidence, yet coupled this with a quiet and refined demeanour. I guessed he must be a little younger than me, somewhere in his mid twenties.

As we chatted it turned out that, despite having a house in the area, he'd never yet taken a ride on the train either. He said he'd been waiting for the right companion... and before I could draw breath we were waiting on the platform like a couple of excited kids.

The journey provided a true glimpse into the past and was everything I'd ever dreamt, and far more besides. The carriages were so full of character compared to modern trains, and we stuck our heads out the window to gain a better view of the countryside whizzing past. Big mistake! From a distance the smoke billowing out looks so pristine and white, but it's actually full of small particles of unburned coal that sting your face. We pulled them back in pretty fast, giggling all the while.

We got out at Corfe and strolled around the galleries, teashops and pubs, stopping for lunch in one he recommended that lay in the shadow of the magnificent ruins of the castle. We had chatted about this and that, nothing terribly consequential, but now I was keen to get to know more about him.

'So, come on, I've told you a bit about my work, now tell me what *you* do for a living? Or are you perhaps a man of leisure?' Judging by his turnout he had money, but maybe it was inherited? He certainly seemed to come from what some would call *good stock*.

'Ah, so you want me to divulge all my secrets straight away!' He laughed, transfixing me with his gaze.

'*Please* tell me you're not a drug dealer?' I too laughed,

although nervously, to mask a slight concern that seemed to be surfacing from my unconscious. Somehow there definitely was something a bit different, maybe a touch *alternative*, about him.

'No, afraid not... although you're lukewarm,' he replied with a mischievous twinkle.

'Thank heaven for that!' My relief was genuine. 'Soooo... drugs but not a dealer eh... hmmm... maybe a doctor of some sort?'

'Warmer.' I was hoping for more but he left me hanging.

'Are you *embarrassed* to tell me what you do?' That's definitely the feeling I was getting.

'Maybe... a little. Look, I'm a scientist... but I tend to avoid going into too much detail because it can put people off.' He was no longer smiling, and if anything was wearing the sort of sad expression that made me want to reach out to him all the more. Plus I was now properly intrigued. He certainly didn't come across as a typical example of his profession.

'Come on. You can tell me. I won't judge, and I'm genuinely interested.' I didn't need to fake my look of sympathetic concern. 'Oh good lord... you're not a *brain surgeon* are you?' I almost didn't mean to say this, it just seemed to slip out.

'Actually that's pretty close.' His voice was quieter while he stared almost apologetically at the floor.

'I'm sorry,' I said. 'I didn't mean to sound so clichéd. Please Zak... please tell me more.' I moved closer and for the first time took his hands in mine.

'Well...' There was a lengthy pause. 'I don't operate on people, if that's what you're thinking. But I do study the brain and how it works. You see I'm a neuroscientist.' He looked at me now, his eyes full of sadness, seemingly convinced I was going to run straight out the door. 'I expect that rather puts you off me? It often seems to.'

'Are you kidding?!' I blurted out rather louder than intended. I couldn't help but notice that the muttering and sidelong glances of a prim-and-proper, middle-aged couple on a nearby table intensified. I'd never much cared what other people thought at the best of times. Besides which, without wanting to be unfair, they seemed just the type of couple who had nothing left to talk about except the people around them.

Why do so many people end up like that? Are they always mismatched from the start? Why do they allow themselves to be swept away by a lust that soon fades, or the first person that comes along after they've been alone for too long? Or when broodiness kicks in, or they're simply on the rebound? Should they have realised much earlier that they really didn't have much in common, and that in time there'd simply be nothing left to say? Please God, don't let us end up like them. Hang on Zo, you're getting a bit ahead of yourself here, you've only just met him! What's more, right now he's waiting for you to continue...

'I'm not intimidated by a man with a brain, you know.' I smiled, quieter now – the wrinklies would have to get their jollies elsewhere. 'Seriously, that sounds truly fascinating and I want to know more. Do tell.'

So he did. He'd studied biophysics and psychology at Oxford, gaining a double first, and was now just about to complete his doctorate in neuroscience in record time.

Coupled with his good looks this was almost too good to be true – yet I had no doubts at all about his honesty, however stupid that might sound after such a brief acquaintance.

It was as if a dam had burst. He admitted he wasn't used to being able to talk about his work to anyone other than colleagues, while I was just soaking up the entirety of his being. He told me with an endearing pride that he was already starting to make something of a name for himself with published papers. A significant element of his research was trying to understand the way the brain perceives what we call *reality*, and what might actually be going on *underneath* our perceptions of an apparently physical world. He mentioned holograms and quantum fields and all sorts, things with which I had a slight acquaintance mainly from friends at college. But it seems he was also something of a maverick amongst his peers in his insistence that the brain itself *isn't* the source of consciousness. I was spellbound, especially by the way he explained complex ideas with such clarity. When he'd finished I needed some time to take it all in before I ventured a response.

'Wow! It almost sounds as if you're coming from a metaphysical... perhaps even a *spiritual*... perspective?'

'Ah, now... we don't tend to use *that* word exactly. But in truth you're not far off... though if you ever quote me on it I'll have to disown you.' He gave a mischievous grin. 'Anyway, that's quite enough of all that for now. How about a leisurely stroll around the castle grounds?'

This time I insisted on paying for lunch and he didn't protest too much, which I liked. We spent a thoroughly enervating afternoon playing at medieval knights and maidens, before an equally pleasurable return train journey.

Back in my room I relaxed in the antique pedestal bath surrounded by mountains of bubbles. I couldn't believe my luck. Zak was a total breath of fresh air, like no one I'd ever met before.

Dinner in the hotel restaurant that night was idyllic and the food, though sumptuous, struggled to gain much of my attention. Afterwards we moved through to the bar, where this time I had some protection. For all his continued obsequiousness the barman looked somewhat miffed that I dared to visit him with a companion, and his mood didn't

improve when, oblivious to his presence, we sat at a corner table and discussed anything and everything. Eventually he came over to tell us he'd be closing the bar soon, but we just nodded and after he left continued talking long into the night. Do you remember me mentioning never having met someone who sees life through the same lens? Enough said.

It was the same when we had breakfast the following morning, before I had to leave to return home.

No, of course he didn't stay the night. He was far too much of a gentleman to even ask. But the excitement of anticipating the time when he *would* was almost more than I could bear.

eight

The sudden decision to give up my job, sell my flat and up sticks to a new life in rural Dorset did raise a few eyebrows.

My family, friends and colleagues were united in their view that I'd gone stark, staring mad. But I *knew* deep inside it was the right thing, so I didn't much care what anyone else thought. I'd miss my friends for sure, but they'd come down to stay sometimes. In any case I wouldn't be completely isolated because Zak would now be there most weekends. Only he understood my decision completely, and *not* just because he had a vested interest.

Even before I met him I'd been reflecting on the messages in the mirror, which, lest we forget, were the major reason for my venturing down to the coast in the first place. I didn't expect to get much further with the first question about who I was just yet, so that remained on the back burner. But already having the answer to the second – that I *wasn't* happy with my life – my attention had turned to the solution. On reflection I think I knew what it was deep down even before I got to Swanage, so that each passing day only strengthened that feeling. I had to change my life completely, and moving to the town – not keeping my job and commuting, but changing *everything* – was the solution.

As for the third question about who I loved... well, Zak was already helping me answer that one.

We talked regularly and at length on the phone, and the more I learned about him the more I liked what I heard.

Having been relatively reticent about his background when we first met, apart from when I pressed him about his work, he seemingly preferred to talk about me. What a change *that* made from most of the men I'd encountered, who would happily talk about themselves all day long, and then some, given half a chance. Perhaps they'd never come across the old sales adage that *listening* is far more important than *telling*. Actually I'm being unfair because in my experience most people are pretty self-absorbed, whatever their gender. I guess the difference is that men tend to take such pride in their accomplishments. They don't seem to get that most potential partners – at least the best ones – are far more interested in qualities like kindness and selflessness, and in their *characters*, than in their *achievements*.

Anyway it soon became clear I was right about him. Despite the seriousness of his work Zak had a definite mischievous streak that he claimed, when pushed, must stem from being half-Irish through his mother – even though he had no accent and had never lived there. Unfortunately he remembered her about as much as I did mine, because she'd died in a terrible car accident when he was only a few months old. His father had been driving, and was left so crippled that he too passed on when Zak was only five.

But in every other respect his childhood was in stark contrast to mine. He was brought up by a maternal grandmother who showered him with love and affection, although sadly she'd passed away just a few years earlier, and with no other family to speak of it was clear he still missed her like crazy. But nor had money ever been a problem because his father, a self-made man from humble roots, had become a highly successful dealer in exotic cars. Home was a fine Surrey mansion, and he'd attended a local private school before heading off to Harrow – this being one of the express clauses in the will of a father who presumably wanted his son to enjoy all the privileges he himself never had. Although an only child and an orphan Zak had been socially well-adjusted and enjoyed every minute of school life, his popularity boosted by being a gifted sportsman. His progression to Oxford had been much the same.

These massive differences in background could have stopped us in our tracks before we'd even got started. But our common ground was to be highly privileged in the brains department, and this seemed to completely overcome everything else, gluing us together right from the outset.

In any event when his grandmother died he sold the mansion, which had been far too large even for the two of them, and with the proceeds invested in two properties between which he could share his time. One a beautiful medieval townhouse right in the heart of Oxford, and the other a country retreat down near Swanage – a wonderful thatched cottage in one of the outlying villages. Guess what? He too had been brought here as a child and fallen in love with the place.

Our conversations also revealed just how serendipitous our meeting had been.

'I wouldn't have been there that weekend if I hadn't been let down by friends in Oxford at the last minute and decided to come down alone,' Zak mused one day. 'I almost always bring friends with me, but something was just telling me to come anyway.'

'It's not only that,' I added. 'I only booked my trip two weeks before, and if we hadn't met when we did I might never have come down again... meaning we might never have met *at all*. I can hardly bear to think about it.'

'But even *that's* not all!' He seemed just as excited about this as I was. 'You see I'd hardly noticed the railway station before. I know it seems daft, but I'm really not very observant.' I would come to know that actually he was often preoccupied with the ideas whirling around in his head. 'So I just happened to be walking to the Post Office that morning, and then I saw you walking along in that wonderful hat. It's really not something I'd normally do, but I had this incredibly strong feeling that I *had* to follow you. I couldn't even see your face. Then when I saw you at the till in the café I nearly got cold feet!'

'Why?' Of course I had this image of him being strong and sure of himself and in control.

'Well... I've never approached a girl like that before.'

'Really? Never? Come on Zak!'

'No... really... it's true.' He was in embarrassed mode again. 'It will sound arrogant, and I hope you realise I'm not like that... but... well I guess because I'm fairly well off... and maybe not *too* bad on the eye... girls normally approach me.' I could tell he was genuinely uncomfortable now. 'But it's almost as if an unseen hand literally pushed me in the back and through the open doorway.'

'Well, whoever or whatever it was, thank heaven they did!'

'Too right!' He paused. 'Actually as a scientist I'm fascinated by how and why and how apparent coincidences of such magnitude in our lives happen. My colleagues all insist they're down to blind chance and complete coincidence... but I'm really not so sure.'

Nor was I. The messages in the mirror, combined with Zak talking about his work, had already resurrected my interest in the more philosophical questions about life that I'd ignored while wrapped up in City life. But this was perhaps one of the most important of all. Had we been somehow *destined* to meet?

Perhaps even more intriguing, had I been somehow *destined* for rejection in my early life? If so, why had Kim had it so much easier? I had definitely rejected the idea of an old man with a fluffy white beard controlling all our lives, and I wasn't going to return to it now. So *who* or *what* had made these decisions, if decisions they were – and *why* had they made them?

nine

As soon as I made up my mind to leave London everything fell into place remarkably smoothly. The bank was reluctant to let me go and even offered me more money and a promotion, which was flattering. But as soon as they understood I was adamant they wished me well and were more than generous with my final bonus. In the meantime my flat was easy to sell, the immediate offer at the asking price from a cash buyer being significantly more than I paid for it. With the mortgage already paid off I was in good shape to look for my new Swanage home.

I didn't want to go over the top budget-wise, because with no job I'd need plenty of savings to see me through. Two bedrooms would suit me fine, because I could use one as a study-cum-spare room combined if necessary, while I also felt it would be good not to be too far from the town centre. Other than that I was pretty open, so I picked a variety from the bunch sent to me by local agents and made arrangements to view them early in April, as soon as my month's notice at work had expired.

One was a very nice maisonette in a modern development past the pier at the southern end, which to me at least was somehow reminiscent of the model village in *The Prisoner* – the cult television show from the sixties that I'd been introduced to at college. On the hill overlooking this at the edge of town a luxury flat on the upper floors of a Georgian-style terrace also had stunning views of the sea, but something still felt not quite right. I saw a few other properties that didn't really appeal despite the agents' best efforts, and by then it was mid-afternoon. I was just on the point of returning to the hotel, ready to take up the baton again the following day, when I received a call from an agent I'd already seen that morning. A charming cottage had just at that moment been placed on the market. With no details yet, the owner had said I could view it straight away if I wanted?

It lay only about a quarter of a mile from the hotel. The agent met me in the lobby to act as escort and, as we turned off the high street and dropped down towards an imposing church, a picturesque millpond quite unexpectedly came into view on our left. On its far side a terrace of quaint cottages sloped down the hill, their light grey stonework and mostly white doors and windows offset by darker slate roofs.

But it was the one at the far end of the cul-de-sac that really caught my eye. Not only was the door nicely augmented by a gabled porch and the windows by large wooden shutters, but all these, together with the guttering and drainpipe, were painted a vibrant, primrose yellow. What's more it was detached from the rest by a narrow passage.

With no sign up yet one part of me hardly dared hope this was the one for sale, yet another part somehow knew it was. Was this destiny again? Whether its houses, cars, shoes or whatever, you might fight your instincts with your head and insist on looking at lots of alternatives, but invariably you come back to what you *knew* was right in the first place.

'What a gorgeous location,' I said. 'I love the pond and the church!'.

'Yes, I'm told it's very rare for one of these cottages to come up, so your timing is perfect.' She was perhaps a typical agent – or even sales person generally – smartly dressed, friendly, but underneath it all somewhat lacking in substance and sincerity.

'So which one is it?' I was trying to sound as casual as possible.

'Let me just check.' She started shuffling through some notes in her bag as we walked down the hill. 'Ah, here we are. It's Honeysuckle Cottage.'

We started walking along the row, checking the names. It was clear this was her first visit to this area – presumably she too hadn't been in Swanage long. 'Not that one.' The tension was killing me. 'Not... that one'. Then finally we saw the wooden plate on the wall of the last cottage. 'This is it.' She scrutinised the bright paintwork. 'How charming!'

Immediately my instincts were confirmed I decided not to fight them. Even before we went inside I knew this would be my new home.

I paid the asking price – after all it had only just gone on the market and there would be strong demand – pushed for an early completion and moved in at the end of May. All my furniture in London was modern, so I sold it too – luckily the new owners were first-time buyers and they jumped at the chance to purchase it all at a reasonable price. Starting from scratch I furnished the cottage tastefully but not extravagantly. I did allow myself a simple four-poster in the master bedroom though – that was something I'd always hankered after.

My greatest indulgence was my books. Of course I'd amassed a fair collection at college, but now I could afford to enhance it significantly. I went to a large bookstore in nearby Poole and spent a happy day ranging through all the different sections, picking out those borrowed from the library that had made a big impression on me when I was younger, as well as others that now took my fancy.

There was a delightful little third bedroom built into the roof of the cottage and, although the front and back walls followed the slope of the roof, I could stand in the wide centre portion. With dormer windows front and back making it nice and light, it became an ideal study. I had the two side walls lined with shelves, while a reproduction pedestal desk topped with green leather, coupled with a matching captain's chair, took pride of place under one window. Under the opposite window I placed a large bean bag. I was very proud of my little bolt hole and its collection. I'd be able to relax in there for hours catching up on all the reading I hadn't done for years.

On the first floor there was a bedroom at the front and one at the back. With the twin windows of the former looking out across the pond to the church, it was obvious which one I would choose as a master. But then I had a wonderful additional surprise on my first night. Generally it was tranquil and quiet, with little road or other noise – apart from the water! Although it hardly flowed at all and the pond was full of weed, as it drained into a culvert right opposite my front door it sounded like a small waterfall. It was magically evocative, and even in the winter I'd leave my bedroom window open so I could listen to it as I dropped off to sleep. The one slight annoyance was the church clock loudly chiming the passing of every hour, but I soon got used to this – and even grew to see it as part of the charm of my new home.

On the down side – after all no property is perfect – I only had a small westward-facing garden at the back and the surrounding buildings and fences meant it received little sun in the afternoons. But in the mornings when the weather was fine I'd sit on my front doorstep drinking my coffee and basking in its glow. On my arrival one of my first priorities was to adorn the front with hanging baskets and a variety of potted plants of various sizes, and their scent and colour only enhanced my sense of peace and wellbeing.

A lovely old Mill House sat next to the cottage at right angles, blocking off the end of the road. Not long after I moved in I was sitting out front when its door opened and out stepped a well-dressed couple in their sixties who came straight over to introduce themselves.

'Terrific to see a bit of colour about the place!' Johnny Fawcett was an archetypal ex-military man: six foot-ish, on the stout side, somewhat red in the face perhaps from over indulgence, but with a kindly twinkle in his eye. The carefully twisted and waxed ends of his bushy, grey, handlebar moustache twitched as he spoke, his gravelly voice booming off the walls. 'The buggers before you were never here and made no effort at all!'

'That's very kind, thank you. I'm making up for my lack of any sort of garden in London.'

'Oh, so you won't be living here either?' said Marjorie, failing to hide her disappointment.

'Sorry yes… I mean no. I will.' I was even confusing myself, my nervousness with strangers still not completely conquered. 'I've sold my place up there, I'll be here full time. You're stuck with me I'm afraid.'

'Well I can think of worse things that seeing a fine young filly like yourself when I come out of ma front door!' Yes he was being an old-fashioned chauvinist, but there was no trace of lechery. It was clearly his way of paying me a compliment, and I warmed to him.

'Johnny, you dreadful, dreadful man!' Marjorie looked as though she may have been fairly long-suffering, but nor did she seem genuinely annoyed, the affection between them almost tangible. She did however seem worried about how I'd taken his comment. 'I'm so sorry for his bad manners my dear.'

'Please... don't be,' I reassured her. 'It's not every day I receive such a charming compliment.' Our eyes met briefly, it was clear we understood each other... and her husband.

'I think we're going to get on splendidly,' she smiled. 'Come on Johnny, I'm sure Zoe's got plenty on her plate having only just moved in, and in any case you don't want to be late for that nice doctor. Goodbye for now... you must come round for coffee very soon.' She grabbed his hand and started off up the hill, while he looked over his shoulder at me, turning down the corners of his mouth in a mock display of subservience.

The other neighbours were friendly too. Indeed Swanage generally was very welcoming compared to the lack of community feel in the parts of London I'd grown used to. With the sea and the countryside and everything else I woke up every day feeling as if I were on holiday.

Yet at the same time Honeysuckle Cottage already felt like home too.

ten

In the meantime Zak was growing to be a big part of my life. We'd been speaking on the phone regularly, and although we only hinted at our growing feelings for each other it was clear they were there. The big problem was that we were unable to meet up – in London, Oxford, Swanage or anywhere else. For much of March and April he was busy travelling around different parts of the country interviewing other neuroscientists in order to complete his doctorate, while in the lead up to leaving London and for a few weeks afterwards I was naturally flat out. But we agreed that as soon as I was properly installed in my new home – about which he sounded just as excited as me – he would come down and take me on a guided tour of the Purbecks.

Thank heaven this turned out to be not long after the move because, despite both of us being preoccupied with other things, by this time we were desperate to see each other again. What he hadn't mentioned was that we'd be sightseeing on his motorbike, and when I heard it pull up outside the cottage I was both terrified and excited. Not feeling the need in London I'd never learned to drive and was little used to being a passenger in a car, let alone on the back of a bike. But, more than that, although our phone calls had been wonderfully relaxed, would I still feel the same when I saw him in the flesh?

As I opened the front door he was still astride it, taking off his helmet. He looked as handsome as ever in his jeans and leather jacket, and when he gave me a quick peck on the cheek it felt as if it had only been minutes rather than three months since our first meeting. I tried to mask my desire to jump straight into his arms – probably just as well with him only balanced on two wheels – and instead did what I thought would impress him most, which was to admire the gleaming red and chrome machine.

'That's a real beauty.' I stepped back and tried to read the badges on the side. 'CB750... *Honda*. Nice.' I was trying to sound as if I'd been around motorcycles all my life, but he saw through me straight away.

'Come on Zoe, you don't have to pretend you're into bikes for my sake. I just thought this would be a nice way for you to see the countryside, it being such a lovely day.'

'Yeah... sure, why not?' He could see my hesitation and laughed.

'You'll be fine, there's nothing to be scared of. But perhaps I should've warned you rather than springing it on you like this? If you'd really rather not I can go and get the car.' He was so sweet about it, and in any case I really wanted to recapture the feeling of being *alive*, and it seemed pretty likely this would be one way to achieve it. So there was no way I was going to let a few nerves get the better of me.

'No, no. It's a great idea, really.'

He seemed pleased as he swung his leg over the bike and stepped towards me. Better still it felt really natural when he wrapped his arms around me. 'It's good to see you,' he whispered in my ear, squeezing me tight. I returned the compliment. Our hug went on longer than most, but even then it felt several hours too short. It had been a very long time since I'd been held like that, and I think he sensed I was reluctant for it to end.

'It looks quite old,' I said, returning to the bike to try to take my mind off his taut body pressing against mine.

'It's a real classic, the first real superbike.' He was clearly very proud of it. 'This one dates back to the mid seventies. It was a rusty old wreck when I bought it but I've restored it in my garage in Oxford... it's very therapeutic to get your hands dirty when you spend the rest of your time in your head and looking at a computer screen. I've brought it down here because the roads are much quieter, but it's not long been finished so I've not had many rides out on it.'

'Well you seem to have done a really nice job.' That was no idle compliment – it looked almost like new. *What other hidden talents does this man have? Hopefully I'll find out soon.*

'Well I did it at least in part as a tribute to my granddad. He passed on before I was born, but I've still got a picture of him standing next to his bike that my dad gave me. Apparently he was a very kind and gentle man, and a very loving father. He even sold his bike, his pride and joy, to help set my dad up in business. Then he died shortly afterwards.'

'That's so sad.'

'It is in one way... but then dad certainly used the money wisely, so that I was born into a completely different life from both of them. I reckon they'd be pretty proud of how it all turned out, and this is just my way of saying a little thank you to granddad.'

My God he looked gorgeous as he contemplated the

bike, smiling contentedly to himself. It hit me at that moment – that's exactly what he was. Content, with himself and who he was. Not in a smug way, but with the sort of inner peace we should all strive towards. *Am I content like that now I've moved? Only time will tell.* He interrupted my thoughts.

'Anyway, what about you? This place is fantastic!'

'Thank you. I'm glad you like it too.'

'Like it? I *love* it!' His enthusiasm was so infectious. 'I didn't even know this mill pond was here, right in the centre of town!'

'Come and see inside, it's just as charming.'

We did the tour. He paid special attention to the four-poster that had just been delivered, saying how cosy that must be – the twinkle in his eye just enough to be sexy without being smutty or presumptuous. Then up to the study, which again had just been completed.

'We've got *so* much to talk about.' He was browsing the books on the shelves. 'But not now. Come on, the day is young and beautiful… just like you.' He was looking me straight in the eye. *A man like him can pay me compliments like that all day long.*

Back outside I tried his spare helmet on for size – luckily it wasn't too big – and he showed me how to do it up. Then we were off, heading out of town on the main road. The bike might have been old but it was still plenty fast enough for me, and several times I was taken by surprise as he accelerated and I nearly shot off the back. But I certainly didn't mind following his shouted instruction to be ready to hold on tighter around his waist sometimes and, once I got used to that, and to just relaxing and flowing with the lean of the bike through the corners rather than trying to fight it, it was really rather wonderful. He rode fast enough when the road was clear, but he wasn't a maniac. Actually wonderful wasn't the word. This was downright *exhilarating*! As a way to feel alive it would take some beating.

We rode through the village of Corfe, then turned left and followed a winding country road westward for about three miles till it rose up the side of the high ground to our right – the continuation of the Purbeck Ridge that started right back at Old Harry's Rocks. There was a sign at the top showing we were entering MOD land, with a barrier that could be closed when necessary. We stopped at a large car park a little further on with an incredible view south across miles of Jurassic coastline to the east and west. Zak stopped the engine and we took our helmets off.

'This is incredible, what a view! Where are we?' The day was turning out to be right up there on my list of days when lasting memories are made.

'This whole area is called the Lulworth Range, the army use it to test tanks and suchlike.' I'd seen large tracks in the scrubland on the north side of the Ridge, and now it made sense what they were.

'I assume we *are* safe here?'

'Sure we are... they shut the road when they're on manoeuvres.'

'Thank heaven for that! Anyway, what was that sign a little while back... to Tyneham was it? Surely there can't be a village in the middle of a firing range?'

'Well now, as it happens there's a bit of history to that. If you look down there...' he paused as he pointed a little to the right, 'you can see what remains of the village. It's only a few buildings now, a small school and a church and a few ruined cottages. It was always pretty remote anyway, mainly for fishermen, shepherds and suchlike, but then in the war the army requisitioned it. They promised to give it back afterwards, but they never did. So it fell into ruin, although now it's been partially restored as a tourist site. I'll take you there one day... but today we have *other* plans.'

'Ooh, I love surprises!' I tried hard to concentrate as he pointed out various other landmarks using the large map at the viewing area, but it was difficult. My imagination kept taking over, and it was on fine form.

'Anyway, come on.' He was pulling his helmet on again. 'It's such a magnificent day, it's the beach for us!' And off went my imagination again, now it had a little more detail to work with.

We dropped down the other side of the Ridge, past the imposing Lulworth Castle that lay on the plains below, then turned left and carried on towards the coast for several miles, passing through the delightful village of West Lulworth with its many thatched cottages. Finally we stopped in a large car park near the infamous Cove, which was surrounded by gift shops, museums and so on.

'Oh how gorgeous! I'm guessing the Cove itself is down there?' I pointed to the south as we removed our helmets and Zak locked up the bike. 'I've seen a few pictures, it looks lovely.'

'Well we *can* go down there... but you might want to save

your strength for *that*!' He pointed at a path leading up a pretty steep hill from the car park, along which a sizeable number of sightseers were making their way both up and down, some of them mere specks in the distance. Having made understandable assumptions about my apparently frail form, it was hardly his fault that he didn't know I could easily master it at a run – and the playful part of me couldn't resist.

'Race you!' Before he could react I was off, passing slow-moving walkers along the way until after only about five minutes I stood exhilarated and only a little breathless at the top. I could see him some way back. He might have attempted to run after me at the start, but now he was plodding his way up like all the others. About five minutes later he arrived. Although he was fit, I guess running up hills wasn't his forte.

'Bloody hell... I didn't know... you... had that... in you!'

'Ah well, there's lots you don't know about me.' I winked. 'Does the poor boy want a sit down?' That was like red rag to a bull – after all, he was a man – and he set off at pace down the other side of the hill with me in hot pursuit, both of us laughing and shouting.

In very little time we covered the half mile or so to the bottom of the next dip, weaving our way past the many tourists coming up and down – some of whom found our joie de vivre infectious, although those who were seemingly hell bent on siphoning all enjoyment out of their holiday were less impressed. We collapsed in a heap at the edge of the cliff, oblivious to the startled tourists around us. Then, as I caught my breath, I realised that there in front of us was one of the most famous landmarks on the British coastline.

'It's Durdle Door!' I yelled. Over millions of years the promontory beneath us had been eroded into a huge natural archway. I hadn't realised this was our destination, and must have missed any signs. But as so often it was even more striking in real life, the various pictures I'd seen failing to do it justice. 'Why didn't you *tell* me?'

'I thought you said you love surprises!'

'Yes, of course I do. I *love* them!'

We were lying close, our faces only inches apart, and as our panting subsided I had a desperate urge to kiss him, despite the lack of privacy. I'd had it before both today and when we first met, but never as strong as this. Yet I wasn't going to make it too obvious, or make the first move. Tradition again, you see. Zak seemed to pick up on my thoughts but rolled away and laughed.

'Come on, surely *you* can't be tired!' With that he helped me up and we began the climb down to the beach below.

The steps were quite steep and narrow in places, and too busy with tourists for us to clown around. Then, instead of following the right-hand fork to inspect the celebrated arch more closely, he pointed to the left.

'This way. It's much quieter down here.' I followed in silence. *What has he got in mind?* By now my whole body was tingling with anticipation as we carefully descended to the pebble beach below, intensified all the more when for the first time Zak took my hand as we walked along, gently squeezing and stroking and probing with his thumb and fingers. We passed a scattering of other people but, after climbing up and around a small headland while carefully staying above the water line, he seemed immensely relieved there was no one at all on the gorgeous sandy beach on the far side. My heart was really racing now, but I was a little anxious too.

'I can't tell if the tide is going in or out. Is there a danger we'll get cut off?'

'It's coming in, but we'll be ok for at least an hour or so. If the worst comes to the worst we can get back up again at the far end.' Taking my hand again he led me along in silence now until we reached an overhang in the sandstone cliff where erosion had created a deep, low alcove – in which we couldn't be seen except by someone right outside.

'Oh, wait for it. I suppose you bring all your women here!'

'I've brought a few friends down this way, but I've only ever come to *this* beach alone.' He sat down in the alcove and pulled me down towards him. He was fixing me with that piercing gaze again. 'You see I've been saving this place up for someone *really* special.'

In that sheltered little spot, by a beautiful beach on a warm, summer's day, our mouths slowly came together. No resistance now. He looked faintly surprised when I pushed him onto his back and straddled him, my assertiveness even taking me unawares. It was Thursday the 10th of June 2004.

eleven

The village of small white houses is perched atop a cliff, with deep blue sky above and even deeper blue sea below. The boy is sitting in a clearing at the edge, looking out, as if he longs to escape. He's dressed in a few scruffy rags and could be around six or seven, although he's so small and slight it's difficult to tell. His face is pocked, his narrow eyes are small with one slightly misshapen, and his nose is pointed. The fates have not been kind. He seems timid and afraid, and when his mother calls he quickly runs home.

She's angry with him but he seems immune, as though it's always like this. She slaps him hard across the cheek and he winces in pain but tries not to show it. She slaps him again, this time over the back of the head, when she sends him off on an errand.

The young man is standing nervously at the altar in a small but ornately decorated church. He seems to be in his late teens. On one side sit a number of well-dressed villagers of all ages – seemingly the bride's family because they keep turning round expectantly. The contrast with the handful of shabbily attired neighbours across the aisle is stark, although it's clear they've done their best. The young man himself has borrowed a dark suit so big he seems to be drowning in its folds. His thin, dark hair badly plastered down, he wears that same haunted look.

Finally the bride appears. She's attractive, tall and voluptuous, although there's no disguising the bulge at her midriff. The reason for the total mismatch is plain for all to see, presumably the result of a drunken mistake, and it's a solemn rather than joyous occasion. Despite his fidgeting and obvious nerves it seems the young man is the only one who may be happy at the prospect, his brief glance as she draws alongside suggesting total adoration. For her part she refuses to look at him at any point in the brief service, and her words are spoken with sullen contempt.

Afterwards the whole village turns out for the festivities demanded by such an occasion, joyous or not. Reluctantly she allows him to lead her in the traditional first dance, but afterwards he overhears her talking to a friend. 'He's such a clumsy dancer... and so ugly! Eugh, I can't stand to be near him.' The young man turns away and walks alone to the clearing at the edge of the village. He stares out to sea, tears streaming down his face.

The man is now in his late twenties but as slight as ever. Despite his scruffy clothes his home is spacious and well furnished, presumably paid for by his wife's family. He's just about to leave for work when he hears her talking loudly to her neighbours as they hang out the washing.

'You'll never believe what he did last night! He tried to force himself on me! On ME! It was so pathetic, he was gibbering away about how much he loves me, has always loved me, and can't bear it that I won't let him touch me. It's hardly surprising with a face like that! And his disgusting, skinny little body! Not like my boys, they're REAL men. And he tried to grab me but it was all so clumsy and I just threw him away. Horrid little man! He'll never, EVER share my bed

again! From now on it's the spare room for him... or the street, for all I care.'

All the man's pent up rage from years of abuse, first from his mother and now from his wife, seems to well up inside him. He rushes to confront her, somehow managing to pull her now considerable frame inside the house – although if she'd wanted to resist she could have done easily. He starts to yell at her.

'How could you be so cruel? I've never given you anything but my love! I've sat alone and wept whenever you sneak off at night to meet your lovers... don't think I don't know about them! But you're TOO cruel! I'll teach you a lesson...' The man raises his fist as if to strike her, but before he can do anything she punches him hard, right in the face. He falls to the floor, blood streaming from his nose. She stands threateningly over him and bends down to speak quietly, right into his ear.

'Do you know what? I'm GLAD I lost our baby. It would have been too awful if it had looked like you. Now don't you ever, EVER touch me or talk to me like that again. If you do I will kill you.'

The man is sitting alone at a small table in the corner of a taverna. He's in his mid thirties and his face is showing signs of heavy drinking as he stares into space, occasionally taking a deep draw on a thin, hand-rolled cigarette. He seems oblivious to the large table of fellow villagers drinking noisily together nearer the counter – until their ringleader, an older man, beckons him over.

'Don't drink alone, come and join us!' Although they're all

locals and he knows them, he gets up warily before walking over and sitting on the proffered chair. They pour him a drink and he gulps it down as the conversation resumes without him. He listens as the men talk of their families. They seem to make a particular point of recounting, one after the other, how their wives do exactly as they tell them, just as good wives should. The man is getting nervous now. He realises he's been set up, but is too scared to do anything except sit in silence. Eventually the moment he's been dreading arrives as the older man turns to him with exaggerated politeness.

'And what about you my friend. Does your wife do as she's told, huh?' The whole table falls silent, but their smirks say everything. The man just sits there, shaking with fear, head bowed. He doesn't know what to say so the older man continues. 'Well now, you see my fine boys here?' He points to three swarthy young men sitting on the other side of the table, presumably his sons, who are now regarding the man with utter contempt. There's a pause before he nods sheepishly, head still bowed. The older man leans in close. 'Well now, they tell me your wife does exactly what THEY tell her when they meet up with her at night. Isn't that right boys?'

His smirk widening the middle one replies. 'Oh yes. She does EXACTLY what I tell her alright.'

The owner of the taverna, drying glasses behind the counter, is the only one who looks at the man with some sort of pity as he knocks his chair over and runs out, the scornful laughter of his tormentors ringing in his ears. 'You lot shouldn't have done that... he doesn't deserve it, poor bastard.'

'Serves him right for being too weak to stand up for himself,' replies the older man as he turns back to his companions. 'To weak men's wives!' They raise their glasses and empty them in unison.

The man is probably middle aged but looks much older, very frail and ill. He's sitting in a chair in the corner of the small bedroom to which he now seems confined, a bottle and glass on the table at his side. He seems to be in pain and drinking at least in part to numb it. Suddenly he doubles over, clutching at his stomach and crying out in agony, but no one comes to his aid.

Eventually he drains the bottle and climbs slowly into bed without undressing. Through the window he hears men's laughter, then his wife's harsh voice rings out. 'The doctor says he's getting worse fast. With any luck he'll be dead by tomorrow.'

As the man closes his eyes a tear slowly forms and trickles slowly down, down, down.

twelve

This second set of dreams that imposed themselves on me exactly a year after the first – that's to say in the week leading up to my twenty-sixth birthday, only six weeks after the move – shattered my complacent sense of peace. I'd been so busy with work, then with moving and falling in love, that I'd had little time to think of dreams or messages in mirrors. But this served as an unsettling reminder that somehow I wasn't off the hook just yet.

I could really sense the pain of that poor, scorned man and, especially as he lay dying in bed, again it felt as though I *was* him. Why was I seeing these scenes, and why were they so terribly lifelike – and, worse still, so deeply sad?

It was even more puzzling that these dreams were in such stark contrast to the rest of my life. By now I'd fully stamped my personality on the cottage, living on the coast in the summer was a dream, and after that perfect day on the beach Zak and I were becoming ever closer. He increasingly stayed down for whole weeks or even longer rather than returning to Oxford, so we could spend more time together. He could work from either of his homes when writing papers, or just doing reading-based research. He even found that working down in the country somehow gave him a different perspective that was really valuable – or at least that's what he told me.

We didn't rush things – after all we were both quite young still. But after a while, especially when we were in bed together, he'd tell me how deeply in love he was, how I was so incredibly special, and how sexy he found me. Usually it had rather irritated me whenever other boyfriends said similar things, but they were nothing compared to Zak. The more I got to know him the more I realised just how brilliant, how gorgeous, how sexy, how passionate, how funny, how kind and how loving he was. What girl wouldn't want to receive such fantastic compliments when tenderly making love to such a wonderful man? I had no doubt whatsoever that I was madly in love with him, and usually I had no problem telling him so.

So why did I struggle to return his sentiments at precisely those moments when we were at our most intimate?

thirteen

Even though I thought I wasn't being extravagant and the cottage needed little essential work, needless to say I spent more on it than I'd budgeted. Nothing major, but it always adds up till it takes you by surprise, doesn't it? Despite that I continued with the plan I'd made even before the move, which was to give myself that first year off to settle into my new life – to read, to walk and run, to explore the area, and now of course to spend time with Zak too. After all I'd worked really hard in my teens, at college and at work, so I really felt I deserved some rest and relaxation for a change.

Yet on the financial front it was also hard to break the bad habits I'd developed in London. It was only in hindsight I came to realise that once you've earned a significant salary, especially one that's augmented by a sizeable end-of-year bonus, you kind of lose your perspective on the value of money. So it was only as winter turned into the spring of 2005 that I really started to take stock of things – and realised I was still spending more like the person I used to be with a highly paid job, than someone who had now been earning nothing for nearly a year. It had to change, or I'd be in real trouble in no time.

'Look, sweetheart, I've got more than enough money for both of us.' Zak had been very sweet in trying to reassure me.

'I really appreciate the sentiment, I really do... but as an adult I've never been dependent on anyone else, and even as a child I earned my keep from a pretty early age. So I've got my own reasons for wanting to remain self-sufficient.'

'I understand my love. I know about how your parents made you feel. But just know that my support is there for you any time you need it.' I kissed him. He couldn't have been any kinder or more understanding.

Of course well before this I *had* given some thought to what I was going to do long term, and there'd only ever been one option that really appealed. I certainly wasn't going to dive back into the rat race – not that there was much of a chance in Swanage, so I'd have been forced to commute to a larger town or city anyway. In any case I definitely wanted to be my own boss from now on. But I also had a strong sense that I no longer wanted to be involved in anything typically commercial. What I *did* know was that I had my good old brain, and I'd studied English Lit at college, and I could do one thing better than most: apart from running a long way, I could *write*.

I'd had articles published in various college magazines – just simple, unpaid pieces, usually about student life – but people seemed to like them and often urged me to do more; and several of my essays had won minor awards for literary criticism. So although I'd thought about trying to be a writer on numerous occasions over the years, it was only now I faced an important decision that it developed into the strong conviction that this would be my future.

But *what* should I write? And *how* would I make sure it earned me a living?

fourteen

The girl is around ten years old. She's sitting on some straw in a shed, watching from a distance as two men help a heavily pregnant cow. One in his early twenties, taller, better dressed and giving the orders. The other appreciably older, his long, dark hair filthy and matted under a battered black hat with a narrow brim, his clothes dirty and well worn over his stocky frame. The girl sits still but is clearly fascinated.

The cow seems to be having problems. The two men have an anxious conversation and the younger pushes both arms right inside, seemingly trying to twist the calf around before he starts to pull. After much straining by both men it slides onto the floor. But it doesn't move.

Its mother is too tired to even turn round and look – she seems to know what's happened. The men walk away to catch their breath, muttering to each other. Only the girl runs over to tend the poor creature, kneeling down and placing its head in her lap. She strokes it and rocks back and forth as if trying to bring it to life. Tears stream down her face, her smock growing wet and stained with the various fluids.

The younger man comes back to check out the mother and, satisfied, leaves. The older man walks over purposefully, picks up the dead calf's hind legs without ceremony and begins to drag it away. The girl tries to pull it back, screaming and shouting at the man, but he roughly pushes her away and carries on with his work.

She lies prostrate... defeated, dirty and distraught... and beats the floor with her fists.

The girl is older now, in her late teens. She's in a stall in the same barn as before, milking one of the cows. The man in the black hat is framed in the doorway, still and silent. He stands watching her for a long time, unseen.

Suddenly he strides over and grabs her arm, pulling her off her stool. In no time he has her trapped up against the wall with his body, fumbling with his trousers with one hand and lifting her smock with the other. She seems powerless against him, writhing and beating his back with her fists but to no visible effect. She's screaming but no one appears.

Desperate the girl turns her head and clamps her mouth around the upper part of his ear. He cries out but is consumed by his lust, while her head stays locked in place. Finally, no longer able to bear the pain and with a great cry of anger and frustration, he violently pushes her aside and staggers against the wall, clutching the side of his head.

The girl spits something onto the floor, her mouth covered in blood. For a moment they stare silently at each other with undisguised hatred, him deflated and defeated, her disgusted and defiant. She gets up, turns on her heel and strides out of the barn. No words are exchanged.

The younger man is pacing up and down in a farm kitchen, although he looks older now, around thirty. The girl walks in. He gestures towards the table and she sits. He looks serious as he bends over her.

'Sister, surely you can understand my position? That man

was with our father through good times and bad, and when he died he made me promise I'd never get rid of him, come what may. I know he's filthy and bad-tempered, but he's a good worker and they're hard to come by. So I can't ask him to leave... I simply can't.'

'But surely you don't believe I attacked HIM? What I did was in self-defence!'

'I don't know what to believe.'

'How could you even THINK I'd want a man like that? He's disgusting!'

'That's as may be, but all I know is I can't do without him, so you've got to decide what you want to do.'

'It's him or me brother. I cannot stay here after what he did to me.'

He walks over to the window and stares out. He remains silent. Eventually she rises slowly from the table, a look of resignation on her face, and disappears from view. Soon she reappears carrying several bags. She looks at him, but he ignores her.

'I've got nowhere to go and I don't know how I'll live, but I'm fit and strong, I'll be fine. Don't worry about me.'

She crosses to the door and leaves without looking back. Her brother watches her through the window, pain etched across his face. He turns back to the table, sits down, lays his head on his arms and quietly weeps.

The busy streets of what seems to be early-Victorian London are teeming with people. St Paul's Cathedral is visible in the background, and in the middle of all the hustle and bustle stands the girl, more a woman now, perhaps in her mid thirties. She's carrying a large basket of fruit, offering it to passers by. When it's finally empty and dusk is coming on she walks several hundred yards to another street, then over to a man whose basket is empty too. They share a few words before walking off together, arm in arm. Despite their shabby attire they're happy.

They enter a nearby inn. The main bar is rowdy and full of other street vendors spending meagre earnings on their only means of escape. The man buys their drinks and they find a small table in a quiet corner in the annex.

The woman looks earnestly at the man and whispers something in his ear. He recoils with what appears to be joyous shock, then hugs her tight, kissing her cheeks again and again. Finally he lets her go and, with an unspoken request that she grants with a tearful smile and a nod, places his hand carefully on her belly.

They finish their drinks and leave. It's now dark outside and they don't see the filthy man, his black hat askew due to the lack of most of one ear, who's been watching them all the while and now follows them down the alleyway at the side. They make their way through the backstreets to the river, emerging at a quiet spot near an old wooden jetty. They walk out onto it, arm in arm, and stare contentedly at the water.

Suddenly there's movement behind them. The woman turns just in time to see the man rushing at them, his face a twisted mask of hatred, but her lover is caught completely unawares. He has no time to react as his assailant pushes him violently towards the edge. Desperately he tries to regain his balance as one arm and one leg flail over the water, the woman powerless to help. After what seems an eternity he loses his valiant struggle with gravity. The man in the hat runs off as she screams for help, but when others arrive it's too late. Carried away by the strong current, after a brief struggle her lover's head has already disappeared beneath the filthy, cold, darkness.

She collapses to her knees and sobs uncontrollably as the bystanders try to comfort her.

The woman is walking down a dark, deserted street at night. The swelling in her belly is now obvious. Gradually she quickens her pace, casting nervous glances behind her. The shadowy figure of the man in the hat is stalking her on the other side. He slips in and out of doorways and hides behind anything available to avoid detection.

Suddenly he too quickens his pace and, crossing the street in a few strides, rushes at her. After a brief struggle she's pinned, petrified, against the wall – just as she was many years before. With a start she recognises him and in close up now he is filthier and more horrible than ever. He leers at her, and she fears he'll attempt the same again.

Instead he quickly places his left hand across her mouth and his right in front of her face, revealing a six-inch dagger. He seems to take great pleasure in turning it to show her the glinting sides of the blade – so clean and new, unlike its owner. Her screams are muffled but her eyes are wide with abject terror. He stares into them with pure hatred, and for a few seconds the two figures are completely still. Could the loss of half an ear create that much desire for revenge? Or was it just that she rejected him? Or both?

She'll never find out. With one swift movement he plunges the knife deep into her side. She's lifted up by the power of his strike and he thrusts it ever deeper into her, his cold, cruel eyes boring into hers the whole time. Her body shudders, then as it begins to go limp he gives the knife a final, violent twist before pulling it out and wiping it on his trousers. He spits into her lifeless face before walking away as if nothing had happened.

The woman slumps to the floor and lies motionless on the cold, hard cobbles. Gradually a thick, crimson pool forms by her side.

fifteen

Again I'd been so preoccupied with my new life that I'd pretty much forgotten the dreams. But in retrospect it came as no great surprise when this third set forced themselves upon me in the lead-up to my next birthday that summer of 2005, and the finale was even more vivid than previously. This time when I awoke the bedclothes were damp with sweat, I could still *smell* the man's breath, still *see* the horrible glint in his eye, still *feel* the sudden, stabbing pain. Again I'd witnessed the final scene through the woman's own eyes, along with the strong sense that somehow she *was* me and I *was* her. But how could that be?

What's more, just as before, the horror of my dreams seemed in stark contrast to my new life, because things were pretty good, especially between Zak and me. Except... For some time he seemed not to notice my reticence in expressing emotion during our lovemaking, especially because in everyday situations I had no problems telling him exactly how I felt. But finally the day came when we were lying in bed afterwards.

'Zo, are you sure you really *do* love me?' It was clear this was hard for him because he'd been used to nothing less than total devotion from previous girlfriends.

'Are you kidding? I adore you!' I wasn't lying, but I didn't want to ask why. I knew what was coming.

'It's just... well, you never say anything when we're making love.'

My heart went out to him, he was genuinely hurt and confused, and I couldn't blame him. But I had no choice but to lie, because I didn't know what was going on any more than he did. 'Oh, darling, that's just me. It's just how I am when we're... you know.'

He seemed to accept this but not long after that third set of dreams something else added to what I now know was a growing sense of imbalance felt by both of us, however much we tried to sweep it under the carpet.

We'd always agreed to take things slow and easy, but our commitment to each other was by this time clear enough that Zak had every right to raise the issue of children. Yet strange as it might sound I'd never really given it any thought, and found myself completely taken by surprise when he said he'd love for us to start a family one day. Not only that but for some inexplicable reason I just *froze*. We were ushering in 2006 with dinner in the luxurious restaurant of the hotel where we'd eaten the night we first met, and I was so taken aback I had to excuse myself.

In the bathroom I burst into tears, and all I could hear was a forceful voice in my head... *No children! Not for me! A woman like me doesn't deserve children!* It took me a long time to compose myself and fix my makeup, so that when I returned Zak was understandably concerned. To my great discomfort I found that again I was being forced to cover up something I didn't understand, and nor could I be sure how convinced *he* was by my airy *I'm fine – let's just wait and see, eh?* on my return. Young he might be, stupid he wasn't.

My dreams and these issues with Zak were starting to eat

away at my happiness, while other issues too were forcing me to again take stock of my life. I'd had a few exploratory articles published in lifestyle magazines, mainly about the change from city to country life, and I even had a small regular column in a local paper. But these hadn't yet led to anything more substantial, and the meagre sums I'd been paid had done little to alleviate the harsh truth that I'd now been without any sort of formal income for more than two years. My savings were depleting fast, and I was really starting to feel the pressure.

Of course magazine articles weren't where I saw my future as a writer. From the moment I'd conceived of this path I'd had a strong sense that I had at least one decent novel in me, and I'd been toying with various ideas for plots and characters without getting a great deal further. So in the previous few months I'd started to instil some discipline into the process, and forced myself to sit at my desk at certain times of the day. The trouble was I seemed to have a pretty bad dose of writer's block – and even when I did manage to type something it soon found its way into the trash folder of my computer.

In February Kim came to stay for the weekend. I only saw her a few times a year now but we talked on the phone at least once a month, and when we got together it was great – she loved the change of scene and had begun to understand why I'd made the move. We were discussing my writing problems when she took me completely by surprise.

'You know what you need Zo? You gotta start thinkin' more positive!'

'Oh really?'

'Yeah! This whole writin' thing. You need to set some proper goals an' start really believin' in Zoe.'

'Whoa there cowgirl! What makes you think I don't believe in myself?'

'I can jus' tell by the way you talk. It's all *ifs* an' *buts* an' you don't even sound convinced yourself.'

'Oh come on now, isn't that how everyone talks? Isn't that just *realism*?'

'Nah... it don't have to be. About nine months ago a girl at work give me this brilliant book. It says we *attract* into our lives exactly what we think about.'

'Hey, slow down sis! It's bad enough you telling me you've been reading a *book*, let alone one that makes you *think*!' Because of our strengthening relationship this sort of jibe was no longer a problem for us.

'Ha bloody ha, you're real funny. But it works though! For example I've always attracted the wrong sort o' blokes, right? You know that.'

'Yes, sure. They've usually been a bit of rough and the sort you couldn't really have, who'd always mess you about with other women. Kimmy, this is hardly news to me, I'm the one who's been going on at you about it for years!'

'I know. But the closer I got to thirty the more I *really* felt I needed to find *the one* an' settle down. Then this book comes along an' I just started to follow what it said. I wrote down exactly what I wanted – not so much how he *looked*, like before, but more how he *behaved* an' made us *feel* – an' every night before I went to sleep I'd see us together in me mind, makin' love, goin' to restaurants an' stuff. An' you know what?'

'Don't tell me! This time you really have met Mr Right?'

'Please don't make fun of us Zo. I didn't want to say nothin' on the phone 'cos I knew you'd just give us the ol' *I've heard it all before*. But it's been a nightmare not sayin' nothin', and I *mean* it this time... Gerry really *is* the one. We've been together for three months and he's nothin' like all the others. He's got a proper job... and he's kind and decent and loving... an' he's even asked us to marry him!'

'Oh my God!! That's fantastic news! How *could* you have kept all this from me?'

'Jus' wanted to be sure 'fore I told you... besides he only asked me two weeks ago. Bended knee an' everythin'. Course I says *yeah* straight away! That's why I came to see you this weekend!'

I threw my skinny arms around her and tried to squeeze her as hard as I could, while the tears streamed down both our faces. I stepped back and looked at her hand. 'Where's the ring then?'

'He could only stump up the deposit right now, but I'll have it soon enough. I'm not bothered. It's him I want.'

I grabbed her again. 'I'm so, *so* happy for you sis,' I whispered into her hair.

'Thanks Zo. That means everythin'.'

We got so carried away celebrating her news – of course the wine came out straight away – that we forgot the advice it had started with. But a few days later a copy of the book arrived in the post, a simple message inscribed inside:

Please just give it a try! K xx

Because there was a fair bit of waffle it's pretty easy to pare down what it said to the bare bones. Apparently all the 'ancients' understood the 'law of attraction' whereby 'like attracts like', and that it's the power of our words and even more our thoughts and intentions that 'creates the reality' we experience. So instead of letting our subconscious, programmed and often negative thoughts rule what happens in our lives, we need to become much more aware of what we're thinking so we can 'consciously create' the life we want.

Of course I'd heard of 'positive thinking', but this was taking it to a new level. It also tied in to the question Zak had raised some time back about *who* or *what* decides our destiny, if anything. Could it really be me, myself, I? I was sufficiently intrigued to try out the few exercises in the book. First it suggested I should think of someone who was always negative and miserable, bemoaning their luck and expecting the worst. That one was easy, father was jumping out of the page before I'd even had chance to finish the paragraph. And what happens to them? They get exactly what they *expect*, in the form of more bad luck – except of course it isn't bad luck, it's what they're *attracting* to themselves. This made good sense.

By contrast what about people who always seem to attract good fortune? Aren't they always positive and upbeat, dismissing anything bad with a quick shrug and refocusing on the positives in their life? I'd never really thought about it before but immediately I read those words Zak came to mind. That was exactly what he was like. In fact on reflection it was one of the major reasons I loved him so much. And what happens to people like that? They seem to be the lucky ones who just keep getting more and more of the good things in life – except, again, it's not luck. It's what they *attract* with their words, thoughts and attitudes.

Then the book suggested I should think about myself and see where I was on the scale between the two extremes, by listing all the areas in my life where I was mainly negative and all those where I was mainly positive. I did and the lists were pretty evenly matched, so I wasn't a hopeless case by any means. For example, despite the few things nagging away at me about my behaviour towards Zak and the whole children issue, generally I was pretty upbeat about our relationship – and in reality too it was still strong.

The one issue really standing out on the negative side was my writing, and especially my failed attempts at starting a book. Here I could now easily see I was giving out mixed messages to the 'unseen dimensions of the universe' where, apparently, our 'thoughts start to mould the physical reality we experience'. Because while I did still have the deep-seated belief that I had a decent novel in me, I also regularly allowed phrases like *I'll never even be able to start it at this rate* and *perhaps I just can't write fiction after all* to float around in my head. Indeed these were also the sort of things I said when talking about my frustrations, for example to Zak – and even to Kim. Of course this was exactly what she'd picked up on and what had made her mention the book in the first place.

Its advice, in terms of how to turn things around and get into *good* habits instead, could easily be summarised as key points I typed up in my own words to stick on the wall.

Conscious creation is a way of life. You must embrace it with total BELIEF and enthusiasm.

If you really feel healthy, wealthy or successful, or whatever you want to be, you will achieve it. So ACT as if you already have.

Goals based on kindness and LOVE for yourself and others have a much better chance of success than those that come from a place of fear.

Start each day with affirmations. These can be very specific if you want but, to give the universe as much scope as possible to fulfil them, Sometimes loose may be better. So perhaps focus more on your ultimate aim or objective – the WHAT – and less on exactly how or when you'll get there.

Phrase affirmations in the present rather than future tense, as in I AM a successful novelist, not I will be. And focus them positively on attracting what you want, not negatively on avoiding what you don't.

Combine affirmations with visualisations. These should be as real and vivid as possible, and don't just see yourself in the situation you desire but focus on how it makes you FEEL, and how others react too.

When negative thoughts arise just dismiss them with CANCEL, and switch to more positive thoughts instead.

If things don't go quite as you intended see it as FEEDBACK, not failure.

Never forget to express GRATITUDE for what you already have.

Although it said that ultimately the sky's the limit in terms of what you can attract, as long as you completely and utterly believe it's achievable, the book's recommendation was to start with a simple exercise that was relatively unimportant – to get some success under your belt and develop trust in the process.

The typical one apparently was to 'order' a parking space whenever required. Of course I didn't have a car, but since I could think of no obvious alternative I decided I'd test it out with Zak's. Parking in the centre of Swanage was ever something of a nightmare, especially in the holiday season, so it was a good time to try it whenever we drove back to my house. And it worked! Every time before we got there I'd make my silent request and, hey presto! there'd be a space not far from home. Given that we usually had to drive around for ages Zak soon remarked on it.

'That's the third or fourth time in a row we've found a space straight away. We've been really lucky recently.' I decided the experiment was at least a tentative success so I'd come clean. Not only that but I wanted to discuss the ideas in the book with him anyway. I couldn't be sure but I had a strong suspicion they might have some connection with his research.

'I know. It's great when the world bends to your command.'

'You sound as if it's deliberate or something.'

'Well, it is.'

'What do you mean?'

'How can I put this sweetheart? I... well, I've been *ordering* the spaces.'

'Come again?'

Oh well, in for penny in for a pound. 'I've been asking the universe to provide them for us.'

'So how on earth do you do that?' I should have known he wouldn't have the standard cynical reaction but be genuinely interested. 'I mean of course I've heard of positive thinking, and of how top sportspeople use visualisation and stuff, but this sounds somewhat broader.'

'Well, I just ask for a space some time during the journey, and completely believe my wish is going to be fulfilled.' I went on to explain everything in the book, culminating in taking him up to the study to look at my list on the wall. He'd remained silent all the way through, nodding every now and then, but once he'd finished reading he spoke.

'This is fascinating. Would you believe we've just started to test exactly these sorts of ideas, but more in the way of seeing how different people are able to influence controlled experiments... for example the supposedly random numbers generated by a computer. We can then measure the statistical likelihoods and see whether something more than chance is at work. So far it looks like it may well be.'

'I must admit I had an inkling that what I've been doing would be somehow related to your research.'

'It really is, and then some. As scientists our tendency is to keep things under strict control, and to concentrate on developing theories before testing them out in the lab. But you're already out there *doing* this stuff, which is fantastic!'

'Well I'm hardly the first if the book is right about the ancients knowing all this for millennia... and apparently it's worked for Kim and countless others in the modern world too.' There was a pause. 'In any case, surely you realise it's what *you* do all the time? You're my example of someone who always looks on the bright side and believes they can achieve anything they want. And then you do.'

'I wouldn't go that far Zo, I do have my moments. But I guess you're right, I've always had a pretty positive outlook and that's usually paid off. I've never really thought much about applying our research to everyday life yet, let alone to my own life or yours, but now you're really making me think. At the very least I'm going to start ordering my own parking spaces from now on.'

'Glad to be of service master.' I grinned and took his hand. He flashed me one of his suggestive smiles, and he was right. We'd been serious for long enough and the bedroom beckoned.

The success with the parking spaces continued, so now it was time to turn my attention to more serious issues. The book said it was no bad thing to build your affirmations and visualisations into a simple meditation routine. Of course I'd come across other books about meditation that often involved complicated postures and carrying on for hours and so on – and, like so many people, when I tried it I found I just couldn't clear the tangle of everyday thoughts from my head for more than about thirty seconds at a time, so I just gave up. But here the suggested routine involved no more than lying down comfortably for five or ten minutes a day, shutting your eyes, focusing on the steady, deep rhythm of your breathing for a while and then concentrating on your chosen goal.

My first mantra was

I am a successful novelist

and while repeating it I'd visualise myself receiving an award, hear everyone clapping and cheering, and really get in touch with my feelings of elation and fulfilment. The second was

thousands of people are
enriched by my work

and I'd imagine the positive reactions of the countless people my words were touching. Indeed it was far easier to concentrate like this than to try to empty my mind completely. Maybe this was more like prayer than meditation but I wasn't going to be put off by semantics – and in fact after a while I found that I *would* spend some time at the end just practising emptying my mind, but without putting myself under too much pressure.

Surely now I had the secret of success I could genuinely concentrate on my first novel. My career as a writer would no longer be stalled on the runway, but could instead take magical flight.

Sixteen

Even after we'd been together for more than two years it was very rare for Zak to do anything that even remotely annoyed me. But if I had one teensy-weensy niggle it was his tendency to provide a running commentary when we were watching programmes or films – and on this particular occasion he was excelling himself.

Not long after our experience with ordering parking spaces he came across a copy of a documentary called *What the Bleep Do We Know?* that his department had been sent by someone involved, and that had apparently been making some pretty big waves in the alternative community. The blurb suggested it was using scientific ideas to show that what we perceive as physical reality isn't really *physical* at all, and that we can manipulate it to create the experience we most want to have. So he brought it down for us to enjoy together.

Except we didn't enjoy it at all. Within no time he was shouting at one of the 'pseudo-scientists' as he called him – a grey-haired chap with spectacles and matching beard. I told him in no uncertain terms that for once I'd really like to listen without his interruptions, but he carried on huffing and puffing anyway – just in case I needed reminding that he didn't agree with much of what was being said. Of course at the end he couldn't contain himself.

'Ok look, I'm no quantum physicist or cosmologist, but I know enough to see that these guys are playing fast and loose with the facts. It's far more complex and less clear cut than they're making out. In fact the whole area of subatomic research is one of the very best examples of the more we learn the less we know and the more questions we have.'

'It sounds like you're just generalising yourself sweetheart.' I did love to play devil's advocate. It meant he got a reminder I was no pushover, plus it did him good to be tested sometimes. I think many of his colleagues were a little in awe of him, despite his relative youth.

'Whoa, no way, I just didn't want to go way over your head with the details.' He was getting his own back, which was fine, this was the sort of game we played regularly.

'Try me,' I goaded.

'Ok, you asked for it. It's like this. There are various *interpretations* of quantum experiments, and one of these is based on what we call the *multiple worlds* hypothesis. In simplistic terms this assumes that every decision we make creates a new, parallel universe that sits alongside every other universe that would've resulted from every other decision that could've been made.'

'Oh I know all about that.' Although by now he knew I was pretty widely read he still raised his eyebrows in surprise, but I carried on. 'For me the idea doesn't appeal. It would mean an infinite yet ever-expanding number of universes all playing out at the same time.'

'Bang on Zo. I like to describe it as *philosophically inelegant*. Some of these guys try to make out that only *major* decisions create a new universe to make it seem more reasonable, but they have no logical basis for this limitation. They don't even try to define what would constitute a *major* decision, let alone who would have to make it. Is it just humans, or is it *any* sentient being?'

'So back to the film. They suggest that each of us can choose the version of the universe that best suits us at any one time, just by focusing hard on that outcome.'

'Absolutely. But what they *don't* tell you is that the multiple worlds hypothesis is only supported by a small minority of quantum theorists anyway.'

'Ah... that certainly didn't come across, I must admit. So does that mean there's a more mainstream alternative?'

'Yes, it's been around for decades and it's still the one with the most support. Have you ever heard of *Schrödinger's cat*?'

'I think I read about it once. Isn't it where you don't know if the cat is alive or dead till you open the box and look at it?'

'And that's why I love you Zo... I should've known you'd know at least half of this already.' He meant it too.

'Thanks sweetie, but that's *all* I know so you're going to have to fill me in on the rest.'

'Ok. The idea is that you only know the outcome of a subatomic experiment, let's say the position of a particular quanta, when you take a measurement. Up until that time the outcome is unknown – it's what we call a probability *wave* made up of all possible positions. Now the mainstream interpretation is that when the measurement is taken the probability wave collapses and the position of the quanta is fixed – in other words that's the point at which it becomes what we might think of as a *physical* particle. The key difference between this and the multiple worlds version is that after the collapse the alternatives *no longer exist* – even as potentialities.'

'So there are no universes running in parallel with this one, which makes it more... *philosophically elegant*?'

'Well, we have to be careful. There may well be multiple *physical* – for want of a better word – universes, or there may even be multiple *potential* universes that we could explore with an expanded consciousness. But if there are they're not infinite, because I'm pretty sure the law of diminishing returns must come into play somewhere. And, more important, in either case I'm pretty sure they don't arise because of the quantum wave function.'

'Ok... it sounds like that's a whole new can of worms you're opening up.'

'It is, and most of it needs to be left for another time. But for now there's one other major problem with the way the film tries to tie our ability to create our desired version of reality in with quantum theory.'

'I'm all ears.'

'Good. Well, to put it as simply as possible, what happens at the subatomic level isn't necessarily mirrored at the level of more complex systems. Think of the example from the film, where the heroine is trying to throw the basketball through the hoop. When she apparently focuses enough to choose the correct trajectory, she's not influencing the way the probability wave of each of the ball's constituent quanta collapses, because its component particles are already bound together in an intimate relationship that creates our experience or perception of a physical ball. In other words it's already a complex system, not just one quantum wave or particle on its own.'

'I can see that. So what she's doing is not influencing the *makeup* of the ball itself, but the way the entire object *moves*.'

'If only my colleagues had your clarity of thought.'

'Cut the bull and carry on.'

'No, I mean it, I really do.' His look told me he did, and it made me feel good. 'Anyway… back to the girl in the film. She's unquestionably using her focused consciousness to influence the physical reality she experiences – in this case the trajectory of the ball. But it's far more profound and complex than they're suggesting, and unlikely to have anything to do with quantum theory. It's almost certainly much more to do with the workings of the brain and the way we perceive the apparent reality around us.'

'Which is where you neurologists come in.'

'Exactly.' Now he'd got all that off his chest he moved closer, put his arm round me and started to relax.

'Makes sense to me.' I nuzzled my nose into his cheek. 'I guess you can't trust everything you see or read, right?'

Kim got married in September that year and Zak and I went up to London for the low-key wedding. Mother seemed pleased to see me, especially with a partner for the first time, while although father was worse tempered than ever we tried not to let him spoil things. Gerry was just as nice and genuine as Kim had described – not as good looking as most of her exes, and a little shorter than her, but clearly she'd finally understood that looks aren't everything. They seemed genuinely happy together.

It wasn't till that night, as we lay in our hotel bed and

talked through the events of the day, that Zak revealed just how foul father had been.

'Zo, I know you warned me the man could be unpleasant, but I never dreamed he'd be *that* bad.'

'Why, did he do something you haven't told me about?'

He hesitated before answering. 'Yes sweetheart, he did, although I'm not sure I should tell you.'

'Oh, he's put me through so much that it's water off a duck's back now.'

'Ok... well, he actually had the gall to take me to one side and warn me against ever marrying you. He said you can't cook, you don't want kids, you gave up a decent job for a pipedream... *she don't know 'er asshole from 'er elbow* was his particularly choice phrase. I'm sorry to say it, him being your father, but what a horrible man!'

I must admit, despite all the water under the bridge, to be described like that by my own father after everything I'd achieved still produced a momentary, sharp pain. But it soon subsided as I lay in my lover's embrace, which meant more to me than anything father could do. 'So what did you say?'

'Nothing... I just turned and walked away. But to be honest if I ever see him again I might not be able to contain myself so well.'

'Well, don't worry, I'm quite happy for us to keep our distance. I'll just talk to mum on the phone occasionally, like I always have.'

'That's fine with me.' He gave me an extra squeeze, then pulled away and leant up on one elbow so he could look into my eyes. 'I don't agree with him, you know. I think you're the most fantastic girl anyone could ever be lucky enough to meet. I'd even consider going directly against his advice.'

He was smiling but I could tell he was serious. Of course this wasn't an outright proposal, but it was actually the first time either of us had mentioned the idea of marriage. I should've been delighted, and one part of me was dying for him to do the whole bended-knee thing so I could throw my arms round him and accept. The problem was we both knew that for him it was implicitly bound up with a desire to start a family – and my inner reaction, every time I thought of the idea of children, remained exactly the same. In fact if anything my sense of unworthiness was getting worse. So as usual I tried to brush it off with a casual, 'Well, maybe one day.'

I could tell he wasn't exactly overjoyed by my coolness towards the idea, although he didn't say anything. Given that he was still having to accept my inability to express myself fully in our more intimate moments, a lesser and more insecure man might have ejected the entire contents of his pram right there and then. But he was kind and gentle enough not to press me, and only later, just as we were drifting off to sleep, did he quietly ask me to reaffirm that I really did love him and see our future together.

That was a no-brainer for me because, despite my inner demons, in all other respects we were so good together and, on the face of it, were still going from strength to strength. 'Absolutely my love. You are the light of my life.'

I meant it, and he knew it.

seventeen

In the early spring of 2007 I sat back and did my annual stock take – and this time the picture looked considerably worse. Whatever the underlying mechanics of *creating my own reality*, it wasn't working out quite as I'd hoped.

Yes I'd finally been able to start writing my novel after introducing the relevant mantras into my daily routine, and by the time we went to Kim's wedding I had a first draft – meaning my efforts were bearing some sort of fruit. Yet when I read it through I knew it was way short of being good enough, so I poured myself into plot adjustments and other rewrites, constantly agonising over whether or not it would make the grade with publishers.

But now I realised that for all practical purposes I was no further along on my chosen career path than twelve months previously and, worse, only had about a year left before the pot would run dry. I could prevaricate no longer. It was time to bite the bullet and send the manuscript off. Did I show it to Zak first, or even Kim? No. I can't say exactly why – perhaps it was fear I'd make a fool of myself – but I didn't want to share it with anyone close to me at this point.

I did the job properly. I researched how to present it, and got the names of the fiction editors at a number of publishing houses both large and small. Having had about twenty copies printed I sent them off – planting a good-luck kiss on each envelope before it was handed over at the post office counter.

Then I sat back and waited. Like most first-timers I was superficially convinced that the offers would come flooding in, but still that nagging inner voice would *not* be silenced. *It's not good enough. You're not good enough!* So I redoubled my efforts with the daily mantras to keep the positive energy flowing.

Then I waited some more.

And some more.

Finally, after several anxious months, the rejection slips started to arrive: *We thank you for taking the trouble to send us your manuscript but we are unable to take it further at this stage. Nevertheless we wish you every success in your future endeavours.* Or similar. In other words *Thanks... but no thanks*. By the middle of the year all manuscripts had been returned, and my positivity was draining away fast.

By now I was no longer seeing my old friends from London either. A few of those closest to me had come down occasionally in the first year after I left, and there'd been a certain amount of telephone contact after that. But truth be told I was now on a different path and we just didn't gel any more. I had to let them go, and vice versa.

Nor had I really replaced them with anything more than casual acquaintances in Swanage. The closest I'd grown to anyone was Johnny and Marjorie next door, who were really lovely. But, given how little I saw of Kim now she was married, there was no doubting I was pretty much putting all my eggs in Zak's basket when it came to friendship as well as love. If anything happened to him – or to my relationship with him – I'd be seriously isolated.

I still felt we were really strong, but this additional

pressure didn't help my state of mind one bit.

In May that year I got a call from Kim. She sounded breathless and excited.

'Zo, I got some brilliant news!'

'Don't tell me, Gerry has seen the light and you're moving down here to join me?' I'd often told her how wonderful it would be to have her close by, but in truth I knew she was a South London girl through-and-through, however much she enjoyed her visits.

'Nah, you know we're happy here.'

'Ok then, you've won the lottery and you'll be able to have *two* houses?'

'Stop messin' about, this is serious.'

'Well come on then, don't leave me in suspense!'

'I'm only bloody well preggers, aren' I?!'

Something inside me just broke. I let out a scream and began to sob so violently I dropped the phone. When I finally regained some control and called her back she was frantic.

'Zoey, what the *hell*'s the matter? I thought you'd be *pleased*?'

'I'm so sorry sis. I *am* pleased for you, really I am. But there seems to be a problem, and it's not going away.' I didn't want to spoil her moment but she was worried about me, and even I'd been scared by the depth of my reaction this time. So I proceeded to tell her all about my terrible feelings of unworthiness every time the idea of having children came up.

'But you'd make a blindin' mother you would.'

'Thank you... but I just can't believe that... and the worst part is, I've absolutely no idea why.' I burst into tears once more, as Kim tried in vain to comfort me. 'It's not just that either,' I blubbed. 'I've got some sort of problem with really opening up to Zak too, especially in bed. You know how much I love him, yet I'm holding myself back. Not physically, just emotionally.'

'Bloody hell Zo, s'not exactly that surprisin', is it? Not after everythin' you went through with mum an' dad... an' me.'

That really threw me. 'What do you mean? You always used to make out you all treated me well. It used to really upset me!'

'Yeah, well... I reckon underneath it all I felt so guilty about how they treated you, while they worshipped the bleedin' ground I walked on, that I just blocked it off. Dad were such a bastard to you... s'pose I was scared he might turn on us too one day... so I just sort o' joined in. But it was all wrong Zo, all wrong... an' I'm so, so sorry I wasn't there for you then. ' She too was becoming emotional, and this made me cry even more.

'Thank you sis,' I said eventually. She'd changed so much since meeting Gerry, and was so much more perceptive than I'd given her credit for. 'But how does any of that relate to me and Zak?'

'Sweetie, you're afraid o' bein' rejected again o' course! *That's* why you're holdin' back deep down.'

I'd never thought about my situation like that at all. But surely it was nonsense? After all I did really love him and I'd told him countless times, and vice versa. We'd been together for three years. We were strong despite my problems, and I wasn't scared of him leaving me. Or at least I didn't think I was.

'No way. Something may be wrong but it's not that. You're barking up the wrong tree Kimmy.'

'Ok, ok, I'm sorry. I just reckon that maybe you might... you know... go an' *see* someone.'

'Like a shrink, you mean?'

'Well... yeah. Lots o' people do these days, no one gives a fiddlers any more.'

'Hey, I'm not a nut job sis, ok?' Yes, I was well aware of my defensiveness even as I said this.

'Look babe, I know, but you've defo got somethin' goin' on, especially with this children thing. It can't do any harm, can it?'

I told her I'd think about it, but I didn't mean it. I hadn't even told her about the book rejections. I was hiding that from everyone except Zak, who was as supportive as could be and encouraged me not to give up on my dream. So yes I had a few problems, but they weren't *that* bad – *and intelligent people like me can work out their own stuff, thank you very much*.

Within a short time all that would change.

eighteen

A pretty, blonde-haired girl of around ten is surrounded by a group of other children of varying ages. According to the sign on the gates they're outside an orphanage for girls and, judging by their clothes, it's the late nineteenth century.

Taller than her, the ringleader taunts the girl while the others shout encouragement. She looks scared. 'Why can't you leave me alone?' she pleads, and it's obvious this has happened before. Suddenly something inside her breaks. She lashes out and the larger girl drops to the floor. The others stop laughing and surround her, their taunts turned to praise in an instant now there's a new queen on the block.

Before she can receive the adulation due a woman bursts through the gate. 'What has happened here?' she demands. The children remain silent while she moves towards the fallen bully, who is just coming round, and helps her to her feet. The woman then turns to the girl. 'Are you responsible for this?'

'But she done start it miss.'

'I don't care who started it… you're in big trouble lady.'

The girl is dragged off, beaten, and left alone in the dormitory with no supper. She cries herself to sleep.

The girl is now sixteen. The scene is a typical cowboy saloon, and she's standing next to a table in the corner at which a number of young women are seated, all gaudily attired. The exception is what must be the boss, a middle-aged woman of ample proportions who has seen better days, and now addresses her.

'So where ya from missy?'

'The city ma'am. I been in an orphanage all ma life, never knew ma folks. But I had to get out. It was all rules an' punishments an' all. I want ma freedom, an' some country air, so I headed west and this here's the first place I come to that I figure I could settle in.'

'If you're gonna do this job honey you'll need to learn real fast. Ya gotta stay sharp and keep your wits about ya at all times. There's some mean sons o' bitches in this town who'll cheat or kill ya soon as look at ya.'

'Yes ma'am,' says the girl. 'I thank ya kindly but I know how to look after myself ma'am.'

'Well, I hope so, I really do. You sure 'nuff got the looks, I'll say that for ya, and I kinda like your spunk. You're hired honey, sit down and have a drink with your new mama to seal the deal. Someone get me another chair!'

Although some of the others smile, several are already muttering to themselves and casting jealous looks in her direction. Clearly it's not just the men she'll need to worry about.

In her early twenties now, the girl is in her room above the saloon. It's lavishly furnished, and she's clearly been successful. As she lies on the bed the local doctor is gently examining her slightly swollen belly. He is an unexceptional looking man in his mid-thirties, but with a kind face and manner.

All of a sudden he drops to one knee, grabs her hand and starts to smother it with feverish kisses. She doesn't take it away. He looks up at her, devotion in every part of his being. 'I love you! I love you I don't know how much! I've loved you ever since I first saw you!' The girl seems calm and unsurprised – this clearly isn't the first declaration she's received. But he's not finished yet.

'Will you make me the happiest man in the world and be my wife?' he pleads. 'I don't care that the baby's not mine, I just want to take you away from this place and look after you… start a whole new life. I know I'm not the finest man to look at, or the most exciting, but I've got money and a good heart.'

The girl swings her legs over the side of the bed and sits on the edge, motioning him to join her. 'You're very kind doc, and I thank ya for the offer, really I do.' Although it's clear she knows how to be tough, her manner now is soft and kind. 'I know you're a good man too, and I like ya… I like ya a lot.' He looks expectantly at her as she pauses and looks into the distance. 'But I'm sorry… I'm real sorry… I'm just not in love with ya.' He looks crestfallen but says nothing. 'Sure I know it might surprise ya, what with me doin' what I do, but if ever I do marry it'll have to be for love. I sure hope ya can understand that.'

The doctor nods, rises and makes for the door without turning around.

Again the girl is lying on her bed, this time cradling a beautiful baby girl in her arms. Singing gently, she rocks her to sleep.

All of a sudden the local preacher bursts into the room, followed by two assistants who rush at her. He's shouting something about 'Children born in sin!' and she has no time to react as the taller of the two men pins her down while the other wrestles the baby out of her grasp before backing towards the door. As the taller man starts to release his grip she instinctively reaches for the shotgun kept under her bed for protection – but as she swings it around towards the preacher it accidentally discharges at the shorter man holding the baby. They both slump to the floor, motionless.

The girl is screaming and hysterical, everything a blur. The parson and the taller man are still frozen with shock as three cowboys who've heard the shot fly up the stairs and barge their way in. As they take stock the parson suddenly comes to and entreats them to 'Punish the murdering whore!'

They seem to need little encouragement. 'She never had no time for us afore... too busy with all her highfalutin fellas wi' money. Well, we'll see about that now,' says the ugliest of the three, grabbing her hair and wrenching her violently off the bed.

They drag her kicking and screaming down the stairs and through the saloon. Neither the boss nor the doctor are around to come to her aid. Some of the patrons look shocked while others shout and jeer, but no one dares intervene. Exiting through a back door they take her out to a stable. Throwing her roughly to the floor and pinning her there, the ugly one is the first to satiate his lust and gain his revenge for being spurned – and he does so as violently as he knows how. Silent by now she's almost oblivious, although dimly aware of his rotting teeth and nauseating stench.

As the last one is violating her the ugly man holds a knife to one of her breasts and slowly, ever so slowly, starts to cut. 'This is what a dirty, filthy whore like you deserves,' he drawls.

Once they've all had her they take great pleasure in stabbing her repeatedly all over – yes, even there – before swaggering off, laughing... but mercifully the end had come after the first few thrusts.

nineteen

By this time my nightmarish dreams really had been at the back of my mind for several years, especially when the previous summer had come and gone with no repeat performance. But this fourth set, following the old pattern of emerging in the lead up to my twenty-ninth birthday, really did shake me up once more. So vivid, horribly vivid, with the same sense of it somehow being me who was raped and stabbed. But worst of all was the sense that I'd killed my baby. My own, beautiful, baby girl.

Yet in truth, disturbing as they were, these latest dreams only added to a downhill slide that had begun several months earlier, not long after Kim broke the news of her pregnancy. I'd gradually become more and more listless and very, very sad. Some days I didn't even get out of bed and, as for writing – no chance.

For a while I thought I'd managed to mask most of this from Zak, but one morning that August he came round unannounced when I was in one of my ruts. I heard the doorbell and him shouting up at my closed curtains but, apart from anything else, I hadn't washed properly for several days. Yet I couldn't turn him away with no explanation, so I dragged on a dressing gown, took a quick swig of mouthwash and answered the door.

'Oh my God, Zo!' He didn't say anything more, just took me in his arms and hugged me tight. Initially I was still numb, so he let me go – or perhaps I just smelt really bad, though he was kind enough not to mention it. 'We need to talk about this, don't we?' I nodded and let him lead me inside to the kitchen, where he made coffee in silence.

Once we were both sat down he took my hands and looked at me with tenderly. 'I've know for some time you were struggling with a few things sweetheart… I'm not stupid, even though you've tried valiantly to hide it from me. I haven't wanted to say anything before now because I so didn't want to upset you… but then again I didn't realise it was *this* bad. I can't see you suffer like this any more.'

It took time for me to respond, but finally I came clean. 'Ok… yes… I *am* struggling.' This was the first time I'd admitted it to anyone, and I burst into tears. Well, that's something of an understatement, because huge, gasping sobs wracked my whole body. I'd been holding this in for too long, not even being fully honest with myself, and now everything was pouring out.

Zak moved his chair closer. 'It'll be alright my love,' he whispered over and over, and held me tight until finally I began to calm down. Feeling a little better for letting my emotions out I pulled apart and looked at him.

'I don't know what to do Zak. I'm falling apart and I don't know how to stop it. The book rejections have hit me really hard, and I just don't know if I'm cut out to be an author any more. I was so *sure*, and there's a part of me that *knows* I can do it, but another part keeps telling me to just give it up. I don't know if I can fight any more.'

'I can see now just how hard this is for you,' he said gently. 'I should've seen it before.'

'Don't blame yourself. You've been wonderfully

supportive and understanding, as always. But ultimately it's down to me to have the strength to carry on and risk further rejection... and right now I just don't know if I can.'

Again he took my hands in his. 'Zo, look, I know there's some other stuff going on too. It's hardly surprising given your childhood. Perhaps you could at least go and see your doctor?'

'What use is *he* going to be?'

'Well, perhaps he could prescribe some medication.'

'I don't want to spend the rest of my life being addicted to bloody antidepressants!' Of course this was something I'd already thought about, and I had strong feelings. 'Come on Zak, we all know that doctors hand them out as if they're sweeties for kids... because that's what Big Pharma pays them to do.'

'Well, you're right that they make little if any effort to get to the real source of the problem... because that takes time and the appropriate skills, both of which tend to be in very short supply. But there *is* something else they can do.'

'Which is?'

He hesitated and looked down at his cup. 'They can recommend that you get more specialist help.'

'You mean see a shrink? A counsellor, or therapist or something?'

'Yes.'

I was shocked. He wasn't giving me an ultimatum – that wasn't his style, thank goodness, otherwise I'd probably have dug my heels in. But now I had the gentle weight of both the people I valued most in the world pressing on my shoulders.

'I'm not sure I need to go that far... but ok, at least I'll get myself a doctor and pay them a visit.' I was very rarely ill and hadn't even bothered to register with a new practice since I moved down.

The following week said doctor did indeed have a purely cursory chat with me before recommending antidepressants – and, despite my strong views about becoming addicted, having taken a peek into the abyss I realised I was actually desperate for some sort of relief. Anything that would pull me back from the brink. So, assuring myself it would only be temporary, I acquiesced.

The pills did help, no question. So much so that within a few weeks I felt ready to return to writing. I read through my first attempt again and it was clear that no amount of editing could save it. Some sections really jarred – which was good, because it meant I was learning and could avoid some of the more obvious pitfalls. So I started again, armed with my painful, hard-earned experience. But I soon found that the pills had also dulled my mental edge, and I was struggling.

Nevertheless I persevered. Something deep inside was keeping me totally committed to my path, even when all the external signs were that I should give up. What's more, although I'd stopped my daily mantras for those few months when I could hardly get out of bed, I started chanting them again every morning – even if sometimes with less belief than I would've liked.

The trouble was, nothing seemed to stop that nagging inner voice.

twenty

Everything came to a head on my thirtieth birthday.

It was July 2008, and tensions with Zak had been more obviously building, not helped by the loss of the mental edge that had been one of my main attractions for him. On top of that, daily mantras or not, my negativity and self-doubt were getting progressively worse. I just couldn't shake them, however hard I tried, and it was really starting to affect him too. Although I knew he didn't want it to, and he continued to tell me how much he loved me, he also gently returned to the subject of more specialist help, several times – but something was still keeping me from going down that route. I guess I just didn't feel ready. I was stuck, and so was he, and I began to worry we were fighting a losing battle.

The final straw came on that fateful night. Because it was my thirtieth Kim and Gerry came down for the weekend, bringing little Alice with them. Now six months old I'd only seen her once, not long after she was born, and that had been somewhat traumatic. So instead of being excited about seeing my baby niece, I felt uneasy.

Yet by the time they came down she'd grown so much that for some reason the uncomfortable feelings were hardly there at all, thank heaven. What's more it was wonderful to see them all again, and I was really looking forward to my birthday meal that night in the place we now always used for special occasions – the hotel restaurant. Kim had even agreed to let Johnny and Marjorie look after Alice while we went out.

The food was delicious as always, and Zak and Gerry got on really well – not having had much chance to get to know each other before then. But for once Zak insisted on champagne, even though we didn't normally drink that much, and as the night wore on it began to take effect. Inevitably I suppose the conversation turned to my plight.

'So what you gonna do next sis?'

'Well, the second novel is pretty much finished, but I'm scared it's not much better than the first. I think I might have to scrap this one too.'

'On no sweetheart, not again?' Zak was really concerned because, although he knew I hadn't been happy with it, I'd hidden just how bad I felt it really was.

'I'm afraid so darling. It's just not good enough.'

Gerry leant across the table. 'I'm not a great reader but why don't you let us take a look? I bet it's much better than you say!'

He was only trying to help, and wasn't to know I'd always had a really strong sense that I and only I would be able to tell when I'd got it right – as Zak knew only too well. 'Nice try mate, but that's a definite no go. She's never let even me read a single word.'

'So I guess the money sitch is gettin' a bit tight now Zo?' said Kim, keen to change the subject and spare Gerry's blushes.

'Bad. Very bad.' Again I'd hidden just how bad, even from Zak, but now it was all just pouring out. 'Pretty shortly I'm going to have to rent the cottage out and move into a room or something.'

'*What?!*' He turned to look me straight in the eye. I'd never seen him even remotely angry with me – apart from passion for his work he was pretty phlegmatic about most things – but there was certainly more than a hint now. 'Why haven't you talked to me about this Zo? If you'll forgive me that's a really stupid idea. You should come and live with me if things have got that bad. I'm in Oxford half the time anyway, as you well know, so it's not as if we'd be under each other's feet. You'd still have your own space.'

'I'm sorry. I've always looked after myself and paid my own way, even from the earliest days, and I'm not going to change that now.' Of course I knew that my fierce independence stemmed from being made to feel I was sponging off father as a young girl, but I'd always tried to avoid discussing this properly with Zak – I just didn't think anyone else would understand my deep-seated need to prove I could look after myself, no matter what.

He said nothing, but it was clear he wasn't happy.

Kim spotted the awkward silence and tried to step into the breach. 'But darlin', surely you could get a job or somethin'? Anythin' to make ends meet while you sort yourself out?'

I guess it was the drink, or the feeling I was being pressured by people who didn't understand. Something inside just flipped. 'Look, I'm a bloody novelist... an *author*! I know you don't believe me, none of you do, but one day you'll understand. This is what I've *got* to do... and that's *final*.'

We left shortly after. I'd made everyone feel horribly awkward and I hated myself for it, even though what I'd said was the truth.

In bed that night Zak asked me what on earth I was playing at. He'd calmed down but I could tell he was seriously unhappy.

'I knew sooner or later this would all come out,' I said quietly. 'And I've been dreading it darling, because I knew this was how you'd react. And I knew I'd have to turn you down, even though what you're suggesting makes perfect sense. I love you more than you'll ever know... but I just can't move in with you. Not yet anyway. I have to stand on my own two feet.'

He turned away and pretended to sleep and I did likewise, but it was a long time before I finally drifted off.

The following morning his side of the bed was empty, but I knew what was in the note on the kitchen table even before reading it.

> Dearest Zo. I just can't do this any more. I love you so much, but this is killing me. I'm so sorry. Z xxx

Of course I was devastated, but I completely understood too. I'd tested his patience so much with my inability to open up properly, my not wanting to marry him or have children, and my negativity and general loss of sharpness since I'd been on the pills. Now I wouldn't even go and live with him when in dire straits. If I'd been him I'd have left long before. He'd been a saint, but I'd finally pushed him to his limits and beyond. Worse still, I think something inside me always knew I'd do that.

For the next few months I was numb. Zak and I had no

contact and it appeared he'd decided to cut himself off completely. I couldn't blame him and, even though again and again I longed to pick up the phone, I resisted. It took all my strength. Occasionally I'd go to a payphone in the middle of the night and ring his mobile. I knew it would be switched off, and I'd just listen to his gorgeous, sensual voice on the message and cry. But I left none of my own.

In the meantime, although I hadn't fallen out with Kim as such on my birthday, the following morning she and Gerry had made their excuses and left – and since then we hadn't spoken. She was probably just as frustrated with me as Zak, and obviously preferred to leave it rather than harangue me. I guess that suited me too.

As I said goodbye to summer I also said goodbye to my beautiful cottage. I'd advertised it privately and rented it to a charming couple from London who wanted it as a weekend retreat. I could tell they'd look after it and left most of my furniture and possessions in situ. The income would be more than sufficient to cover the rent on my new abode, with a reasonable amount left for food and so on as long as I was careful.

Said abode was a small bedroom in a former council house on an estate on the edge of town. Oh how the mighty are fallen! The couple who owned it were lovely, quiet people if a bit rough and ready – and they had no kids, which would be ideal if I wanted to concentrate on writing again.

Or that's what I thought till I moved in and discovered the family next door were the neighbours from hell. It was an unusually hot autumn but, even with my bedroom window that overlooked their back garden shut, and a fan installed, the word *nightmare* doesn't even come close.

An aggressive, neurotic woman in her forties lived there with her three equally aggressive and neurotic teenage daughters, and I knew their entire family history with all its problems within about a week. It seemed her *fucking bastard* of a husband had done a runner some years back, leaving her to raise her girls alone – although I have to say it wasn't long before I felt a strong sympathy for him. She'd then turned to dealing in drugs to supplement her benefits. So not only were cars arriving outside at all hours of the day and night, but none of them ever seemed to sleep. Their screaming rows went on pretty much 24-7, combining with the loud, thumping rap music that came straight through the wall from the eldest daughter's bedroom.

Can you imagine just how mad it drove me? I thought I might at least be able to come up with an outline for my third attempt at a novel, but instead I just sat in front of my old laptop – perched on the tiny dressing table next to my single bed – and cried my eyes out. *There's no way I can even sleep here, let alone write!*

I had little to do with my landlord and landlady, who kept themselves very much to themselves. We had agreed I wouldn't join them for meals – I had a microwave in my room and ate sparingly anyway. Nevertheless they were understandably sheepish when I confronted them. They explained that any attempt to silence the neighbours had only produced volleys of abuse, threats of violence and, on one occasion, a deep, keyed scratch all down one side of their car.

As angry and sad as I was, the more understanding side of me couldn't blame them for not mentioning the noise. They were desperate for the rental money, and to be fair it wasn't quite so bad in other parts of the house. But mine was the only spare room they had, and was where it was at its worst. Given that one of the conditions of me getting it so cheap was paying three months in advance, I was stuck for that long at least.

But then, as the days and weeks slipped by, the serious downward spiral really began in earnest. It was much worse than the first time. Given that the pills were supposed to be dulling my emotions, I dread to think how I'd have been without them. But nor was I prepared to ask the doctor to up the dose because, however bad things got, the idea of becoming a complete zombie was anathema.

So I simply stayed in bed day after day. Sometimes I could raise the energy to read – I'd never stopped being a voracious reader, still of anything and everything, and there was a well-stocked charity bookshop in the town. But the rest of the time I just lay there staring at the walls or ceiling, endlessly pondering my miserable life.

Sometimes I focused on the general...

I know all about creating my own reality, but something is obviously wrong.

There's no point in chanting mantras any more, they just don't work for me.

I've been especially chosen by the gods, who are clearly against me for some reason.

It must be my purpose in this world to suffer.

I'm a helpless victim in every single part of my life.

Other time I'd give myself a nice change and concentrate more on specifics...

I live in a shitty room in a shitty house in a shitty neighbourhood.

I have no social life because I've lost all my friends.

I have no family to turn to... father hates me and the rest don't understand me, which is nearly as bad.

I have no partner... I've pushed away the one man I truly loved, and now I've lost him.

I have nothing.

And always and forever the fundamental question that underpinned all my thoughts lay in wait for me...

Why not just stop the never-ending, searing pain?

But I was too much of a coward even for that.

Which just made me feel even worse.

twenty one

Since I'd moved out of the cottage Johnny and Marjorie had kindly insisted I have supper with them once a week – *to make sure you get at least one decent meal* was how she put it – but I knew they were worried about me more generally, and wanted to keep an eye out. They were so kind and never put pressure on me, so initially I was really glad to have their company, even if it was painful to see the cottage, and to know I couldn't sleep in my beautiful bed and listen to the water flowing outside. *At least not right now. Hang onto that thought Zo.*

But as time wore on and my depression deepened it became harder to drag myself out of bed to meet them. Most of the time I did it, only occasionally making excuses, because I knew deep down that this one dose of sanity was about the only thing I had to cling on to and to keep me from going over then edge. Yet, just as with Zak the first time my depression took hold, I was too stubborn and too proud to properly admit what was going on – and each time made a real effort to look half decent and to talk as if everything was ok. After all, I'd had enough practice at not showing my true feelings as a child. I think they knew I was hiding things from them, but they continued to show understanding and to not pressurise me to open up if I didn't want to.

It wasn't till early December that I finally cracked. With Christmas coming up I was feeling especially vulnerable and could hold it all in no longer. I just blurted everything out, no holds barred, and then collapsed in tears. Despite being from a generation normally reticent about undue emotion, both Marjorie and Johnny were visibly affected – and for the first time ever she put her arms around me and held me tight. Boy did I need that, although of course my sobs intensified.

When I finally calmed down she let me go and sat back down on her chair. 'We've realised something wasn't quite right for some time Zoe dear, we just didn't want to intrude.' She hesitated. 'But now perhaps we can make a suggestion that might help?'

'Of course Marjorie, you know I trust you two.'

'Well, we've mentioned our daughter Chloe to you before... I think you met her briefly some time back when she was visiting?'

I thought for a moment, trying to clear my head. 'Yes... yes I did. She's a bit older than me... short, dark hair if I recall correctly?' They nodded. 'I really liked her... she had a wonderful, calm energy. Just like her parents.' I forced a weak smile.

'Thank you dear. Well we didn't like to mention it before, but she's also a highly qualified therapist... except what she does is a little unconventional.'

I'd always rejected the idea of therapy before, while more recently I hadn't been in a fit state to even consider it. But now, forcing myself to think straight, I knew I had nothing to lose. 'Go on... I'm open to anything right now.'

'Well, it's called regression therapy. Have you ever heard of it?'

'Vaguely,' I said, but something was nagging at me. 'Oh... is that when they take you back into your childhood, for example?'

'Yes, that's it!' Johnny was eager to get in on the act.

I was still wracking my brain, which was operating somewhat slowly as usual, till it came to me. 'I don't mean to be rude, but isn't that what happened some years back with all those children who claimed to have been sexually assaulted, so they took them away from their parents? *False memory syndrome* I think they call it?'

Before I could say anything more Marjorie interjected. 'I don't know about that dear, but she tells us she gets some amazing results with people who've sometimes been in more conventional therapy for years. She's even shown us a few of their thank you letters, and they're really touching.' There was no hint of disappointment or frustration in her voice. 'Anyway, we just thought we'd plant the idea so you can make of it what you will... but we're certainly not going to fall out about it, are we?' They both smiled.

'Absolutely not,' I replied. She went to fetch one of Chloe's business cards, which revealed she was based in Poole, a mere bus ride away. But as I cycled home I didn't think I'd be paying her a visit. The last thing I wanted right now was to be reliving stuff from my dysfunctional childhood – especially if there was a chance any of the memories might be false.

At supper a week later I told them I was still thinking about it, which was a lie, but they said Chloe and her husband Greg were coming over for Christmas lunch and would I like to join them? After protesting that I couldn't possibly intrude and being told not to be so silly, to my great surprise I agreed. When I got home I realised that, for all that I didn't really want to be with other people in the state I was in, being with Johnny and Marjorie was different and made me feel... well, *loved* I guess... and I so needed that spark in my life, it was the one thing keeping me going. On top of that, as Christmas drew near thoughts of Zak were making life especially painful. Plus it would be nice to see Chloe again, and maybe have a chat about her work. Even if I was pretty sceptical, it couldn't do any harm.

After a scrumptious lunch – despite my poor appetite at that time, even I had pushed the boat out over three delicious courses – she and I were rather obviously left alone for a while. Just as before I found her presence somehow made me feel relaxed and comforted, and I automatically started to open up before reminding us both that I genuinely didn't want to burden her with my troubles when she was relaxing. Yet she insisted it was no problem, and I could tell she meant it. So I told her everything... about my childhood, my real mum, my father, my problems with Zak, my failure as a writer, my depression... everything... even about my dreams and the messages in the mirror.

Chloe was so patient that I only realised I'd been talking for an absolute age when Marjorie popped her head round the door to announce tea would soon be ready. 'I'm so sorry,' I said. 'I'm not normally so self-absorbed, what with this being Christmas Day too.'

'Please Zoe, no need to apologise. You've been through a hell of a lot.'

'Yes but you have to listen to this sort of stuff all the time... probably from people who've had it a lot worse than me.'

'Don't be so hard on yourself. There's no use in comparing your situation to anyone else's. *Your* pain is *your* pain, and it's very real. It really makes no difference if anyone else's is more or less. It doesn't stop you hurting, does it?'

'I suppose not. But it makes me feel worse that I feel as bad as I do when there must be lots of other people worse off. I feel selfish.'

'Nearly everyone feels like that Zoe. But it doesn't help. How about you just *allow* yourself to be in terrible pain... and then you might also allow yourself to try to do something about it.'

I paused to think. This made so much sense. *You've been feeling so guilty about feeling shit that you've even made yourself believe you don't deserve any help!*

'Wow... you're *so* right. You've opened my eyes already. Thank you so much Chloe.'

She looked me in the eyes, exuding kindness, calm and support. But when she spoke it was with just a hint of firmness.

'So when do you want to start?'

twenty two

Not long after the new year dawned I found myself taking the bus and ferry to the therapy centre where Chloe worked. We had briefly talked money and her charges were very reasonable – maybe they were 'mates rates', I don't know. She also assured me we shouldn't need too many sessions, so I knew I had enough put away, especially given that this might be just about the most important investment I'd ever make. For the first time in months I also felt something only vaguely remembered from the past. *Hope*.

I was pleased to see that her room, while comfortable, was plainly furnished and professional – with none of the stereotypical crystals, new age music, incense and so on that I knew would've put me off. Instead the certificates on the wall showed she had a psychology degree, and was fully qualified as a counsellor and regression therapist. That put me more at ease straight away.

After a few pleasantries and her filling out a form about my background, medical history and so on, we discussed what would happen. 'I'd like to start by just experimenting with a bit of hypnosis Zoe, to see how easily you go into trance. How much do you know about it?'

'Only what I've seen on television and so on, when people are made to start barking like dogs and all that carry on. I'm sure you wouldn't want to make a fool of me, but I really wouldn't be comfortable with giving up control like that.'

'Please don't worry. Sadly most people's exposure to hypnosis is exactly that, but in a therapeutic context it's quite different. The people you see being controlled in those shows have effectively given their consent to be made fools of just by attending. And the bit you don't see is the hypnotist doing various tests on the entire audience at the beginning, to establish which people are so susceptible they go into deep trance straight away and can't remember what happened when they come out of it. We'll be working at a totally different level.'

'Do you mean I'll be able to remember everything that happens?'

'Absolutely. I rarely use deeper levels of hypnosis, and even when I do the client's conscious brain is observing all the time and would rebel if it felt uncomfortable about anything. It's also all about *intention* more than anything else and, while the stage hypnotist is there to entertain, we're here to heal.'

'Do you mean intention in the same way as when we use positive thinking and so on?'

'Absolutely! So what do you know about that?'

I explained that I'd studied how to deliberately manifest things I wanted some time ago but that, while I'd had some early successes, the whole thing had now hit the rocks.

'Don't worry, that's one of the things we're going to fix. Sadly they don't tell the whole story in many of those self-help books about attracting wealth, love, the perfect body and all the rest. I'm sorry to be so candid but it really hacks me off, because the underlying ideas are spot on... we *do* create our own reality. It's just that it isn't always a *conscious* process. Quite the opposite in fact.'

'So is that why my efforts at being a successful writer have been failing... and why I seem to have sabotaged my love life too? Is it because somehow I don't really believe I'm good enough or something?'

'I'm afraid so, yes... that's pretty likely to be what's happening. It's the reason why so many people struggle to attract the things they desire. They read these books, which fill them with hope of a better life, but then their efforts don't work – or not long term anyway – and they end up not only disenchanted but usually more damaged than before they started. They think they were somehow deficient in applying techniques that they're told work for everyone else... and so on.'

'That's exactly what happened to me.'

'I understand Zoe, and I sympathise. As I said it really annoys me, because it gives the whole concept that we create our own reality a bad name and people start to reject it en masse. When in fact it's as fundamental to our lives as eating or breathing. We are creating our own reality *all the time*, via our thoughts, beliefs, intentions and so on – it's just we're often not aware of it. There are some writers who do talk about this properly – Anton Wali's *The Power of You* is a particular favourite of mine, I'll give you the details later so you can grab a copy, or I'll lend you mine.'

'That would be great, thank you.'

'Books aside though, the plain fact is that what we believe at a *subconscious* level probably has more influence on our ability to manifest outcomes we desire than anything we chant as a mantra or visualise on a conscious level. So if blockages exist in our subconscious that are in direct opposition to our conscious desires, they'll almost certainly win.'

'So we need to unearth and clear my blockages then?'

'Precisely... and that's where hypnosis comes in.'

'So are you going to *regress* me and make me relive my childhood?'

'I can understand you having some concerns about that, it's perfectly natural. But just remember that we'll be in control of anything that comes up. I can pull you out of trance at any time.'

'What about false memories?' I asked, remembering my conversation with her parents. 'How likely are they to arise?'

'Good question... I know some people remember the bad press regression received because of this some years ago. All I can tell you is that it only tends to happen when the therapist is *leading* the client by putting ideas in their head via their questions and so on. A good therapist never does that... and, trust me, I'm a good therapist.' She smiled.

I could tell she wasn't being arrogant, just honest. 'Well, that's certainly a relief.'

'Having said all that, it *is* true that we usually need to go through the genuinely painful aspects that you may have blocked from conscious memory, and let everything out as it were, because only then can we heal them. But it's all perfectly safe because the intention is right and in line with your highest good.'

'Ok, I can see that. So what happens next?'

She asked me to take off my shoes, recline on the couch, shut my eyes and concentrate on my breathing... in... and out... in... and out. She then told me to focus on relaxing all the muscles in my body in turn, starting at my head... and face... then my neck... and shoulders... easing out any tension... and all the way down my arms... into my fingers... all down my back and spine... relaxing more and more... down my chest and stomach and hips... and into my legs... right down my legs and into my toes... just relaxing and letting everything go. Her voice was so calm and soothing I could feel myself drifting ever deeper, all my everyday worries forgotten. I'd never felt so peaceful in all my life – except perhaps for when I was up on the Purbeck Ridge, or lying in Zak's arms after we'd made love. It was worth paying just for this.

At this point she told me we were going to work backwards in my life in roughly five year intervals, starting with anything that stood out from when I was around twenty-five. That was easy, it had to be meeting Zak. She asked me to describe what he and I were wearing, then the inside of the railway carriage café – and I was amazed to hear myself quietly describing details about the décor and so on I'd never have consciously remembered.

Next my trance-mind honed in on a sunny, summer day in my first year at university, when a whole bunch of us were enjoying a barbecue in the local park. This was nothing special on the face of it, and consciously I'd forgotten all about it years ago, but as I relived it now in full detail I realised just how happy I'd been that day. Surrounded by good friends, entirely wanted and part of the gang, I was no longer a lone outsider who didn't fit in. It felt *really* good, and Chloe encouraged me to linger with the memory so I could drink in the positive energy.

Going back to the age of fifteen was rather different as I found myself being berated by father. I'd been sent home early from school for some minor infringement – I think I'd left my sports kit at home or something – and all the usual insults were pouring forth in a stream of bile: 'You're a complete waste of space... you'll never amount to anything... you're a total drain on the rest of us', and so on. It felt so real as she asked me to focus in on my surroundings that the tears started to well up, and several times I was unable to speak for a while as I relived the horror of such abject rejection without my original barriers in place. More or less the same happened around age ten, except this time my sister and mother were there too and the emotions were intensified.

But the scene that stood out most was the one when I was around five and mother was telling me she wasn't my real mum. I'd consciously remembered the gist of this episode, but now new details were emerging that I'd clearly blocked. I relived it all as she told me how father had been a lovely man till I turned up, but then he'd changed; how he'd come from a really poor background as one of ten brothers and sisters, not all of whom had survived; and how he'd promised himself and her they'd only ever have one child, to make sure he could earn enough to look after it properly.

Now it was clear to my adult self just why he'd been so bitter about my arrival, and had blamed everything on me. But I also relived how at the time – even if mother was just being clumsy and didn't mean to hurt me so terribly – I ran up to my room in floods of tears, jumped into bed, pulled the covers over my head and whispered again and again through chest-wrenching sobs: *I'm no good... no one wants me... I wish I was dead.*

Although this was clearly distressing for me Chloe deliberately let me feel the pain of my loneliness for a little while, but then asked if I'd like 'Big Zoe' to go back and talk to 'Little Zoe'. That felt right, and she encouraged me to just say whatever came to mind. 'You poor, poor little thing. You never deserved even one moment of this. It's not your fault sweetheart. It's not your fault.'

I know all this might *sound* trite and contrived, but when I was in that experience it was incredibly powerful, and the adult me was now crying too. I could sense Little Zoe softening and feeling comforted, and just let that sink in before carrying on. 'You're special Little Zoe... incredibly special... and nothing and no one can change that.' I felt her softening some more, but with the intense emotions being generated I was struggling to continue.

'Just take your time,' Chloe reassured me. 'Make sure you tell Little Zoe everything you want to tell her. Everything that Big Zoe knows about the reality of what happened, and how unfair it was.'

Again it felt right to say more so I did as instructed. 'My wonderful, sweet Little Zoe. You're just an innocent little girl. You should never, ever have been made to feel that you were at fault and unwanted. You are a beautiful little soul that suffered so much for so long. But no more.' I could feel something shifting in both Zoe's now as one comforted the other. Perhaps unsurprisingly, Big Zoe was getting angry.

'I *am* special. I *am* innocent. It's *not* my fault. How *dare* you make me feel like that! I'm beautiful... I'm lovely... I *deserve* to be wanted... *I deserve* to be appreciated... I'm *good enough* to be *anything* I want to be!' I was shouting now but I could still hear Chloe urging me on.

'I'm lovable... and I deserve to be loved!'

I lay on the couch, still panting from the emotion and effort, as Chloe gently guided me back to the here and now and handed me some welcome tissues. She waited until I was calm and properly *back in the room* before suggesting I sit up and take a few sips from the glass of water she'd placed on the floor.

'So how do you feel?' she asked.

'Wow!' I said. She gave me time. 'That... that was pretty *intense.*'

'That's good Zoe. You did really well. We want it to be intense... that's how the healing works. If you're not really feeling it it's not effective.'

We didn't speak much more. I couldn't really talk, and she said that was normal. But what I did know was that she'd undoubtedly started to turn my life around – or, as she insisted, had helped *me* to start turning *my own* life around.

Instantly feeling lighter and more uplifted, I started to wean myself off the pills. I'd have preferred to stop straight away but I knew that could be dangerous. Nevertheless I cut my intake down far more rapidly than would normally be advised. The thing was, people who are clinically depressed often feel completely confused, even guilty, because there's no obvious reason for it. They may have a fantastic family, home and career, so why do they feel so ungrateful and utterly miserable? That must be truly horrid for them. But by contrast I understood exactly what had caused my descent. I knew what I wanted to be, I knew deep down I had so much to offer – as a writer, as a lover, everything. It just hadn't been coming out properly, and one way or another I'd then managed to lose everything. But now I was starting to exorcise my demons there was no reason to remain on medication for any longer than absolutely necessary.

Starting my second session with Chloe the following week with a much clearer head, I was bursting with questions I'd been pondering in between. Not least the most obvious one. 'Was what real I experienced last time real?'

'As always Zoe it's not for me to say, it's *your* opinion that counts. But, first things first, what matters most is whether you *feel* better.'

'I do, seriously better... but I'm still fascinated to know. It's been on my mind all week.'

'Perhaps you should stop *thinking* about it and just go into your heart. What does it tell you?'

I stopped my whirring brain for just a moment and there was the answer. 'It *was* real.' I smiled sheepishly.

'There you are then. It *felt* way too real for you to be making it up, didn't it?'

'So do you think I'll be able to write properly now that I know deep down I'm not a waste of space?'

'Again, what do *you* think?'

'Well, I've started at least *thinking* about plots again, so I guess that's a good sign... but only time will tell if I can come up with that best-seller!'

'Now don't start limiting yourself again!' said Chloe, and we both laughed before I carried on.

'I'm still fascinated to know why I was able to overcome all that adversity at the beginning of my life and be successful in my twenties, and it only came back to bite me more recently?'

'That's not easy to answer, because everyone is different. Maybe your intelligence helped you to breeze through university and your job at the bank and, combined with your looks and charm, it was enough for Zak to fall in love with you too. But then these deeper issues started to emerge and, him aside, it was your writing they most infected.'

'That makes sense. But what about my inability to open up to him properly? Don't we need to do some work on that?'

'Possibly. But it's equally possible that it was simply your deep-seated defence mechanism for a classical fear of rejection. It would hardly be surprising, given your upbringing.'

'That's exactly what my sister said.' I pondered for a moment. 'But all this stuff about rejection still doesn't explain my attitude towards children. What's *that* all about?'

'Shall we try to find out?'

After a few breathing and relaxing exercises she instructed me gently but firmly to focus on the recurring thought I'd told her about at Christmas: *a woman like me doesn't deserve children*.

This time I was instantly transported to a time when I was even younger, just a toddler, and still with my real mum. She was sat on a chair with me in her lap. At last I had an image of her, and she was so *beautiful* – much more so than me, even though I was pleased to see some similarity. She had long, wavy, jet-black hair and, most striking of all, gorgeous blue eyes. But they were glassy and she was troubled... terribly troubled. Rocking back and forth, and looking down but not really seeing me, she was quietly chanting to herself: 'I can't do this. I don't deserve you. I'm not good enough to be a mother. *A woman like me doesn't deserve children...*'

There was a pause as we both took on board the fact I'd only been echoing my real mum's thoughts about herself. Then Chloe asked me if there was anything else I needed to see. Just as I was about to say I didn't feel like there was, I had a different glimpse of her beautiful face staring into mine... her eyes so, so sad and tears streaming down her face onto mine as she held me in her arms.

'Why is she so sad?' asked Chloe. But, try as I might, I just couldn't come up with an answer.

Going into our third session I was confused. 'Although it was pretty intense again, we didn't really get to the bottom of why I've always felt so unworthy of having children last time. Just because my mum did, why should I too?'

'Well, our subconscious soaks up everything it hears, even from the youngest age... even in the womb. So I can only assume that yours took on your mother's constant laments and decided to mirror them.'

'And you think that just because we've now brought this aspect out into the open it will be enough to heal it?'

'Quite possibly... I've seen stranger things happen. I

suggest we just wait and see, and if the problem persists we can work on it some more.'

'That sounds reasonable.' But I had an equally burning question. 'So if all the stuff I've relived about my childhood is real, where does that leave my dreams? Do they have any basis in reality? After all they weren't like normal dreams at all… they felt incredibly real.'

Although we'd discussed them briefly at Christmas, she asked me to run over the details of each one again, making notes as we went along. When I'd finished she sat back and thought for a moment before responding. 'Well, it seems to me there's a pretty clear pattern emerging in all four of them.'

'Yes… they've all been about rejection.' That much I'd already worked out. 'In the first two I was rejected in love, and never had the strength to deal with that but just caved in for the rest of my life. Then in the third I was rejected by my family but found love some years later, only for that to be taken away and then my own life to be cut short. While in the fourth I was rejected from the outset, just as I was in this life now, and I fought my way out of that but again my life was cut short.'

'Ok, that's all fine and right as far as it goes… but here's the fascinating bit. Why were you using the term *I* when talking about the main protagonist in each set of dreams?'

'Because it actually felt like I *was* them at the time, especially towards the end of each sequence when they were at their most intense.'

'Right… and that's quite understandable. But what do you think they signify then?'

'I don't know... they were so scary I tried to forget them, so I've never really thought about it. I suppose maybe they could have been *past lives* or something?'

'Ah, now we're getting to the crux. So did they feel like that to you?'

I pondered this before responding. 'I'm not sure. In one way yes... but in another no. If I'm being completely honest it almost felt as though they were lives that are somehow *still going on* alongside mine.'

Chloe leaned right toward me. 'Go on... tell me more.'

'Well, now I really think about it, it was as if these were somehow other aspects of me that were reaching out to me... maybe even looking for my help in some way?'

'I'm astonished... you are truly wonderful Zoe... you don't need my help at all.' She was smiling broadly. 'Most of my clients who've had experiences like yours... either in dreams, during hypnosis or whatever... tend to automatically assume they're *past* lives. As would many regression therapists I know for that matter. But I'm not sure that's the right way to look at it.'

'Does it make any practical difference?'

'Yes... actually it makes a huge difference, and I'll explain why in a moment. But first there's a purely theoretical problem with looking at things that way.'

She was just about to explain when I couldn't help but interject. 'Which is that time doesn't really exist... so there can't really be any such thing as a *past* life?'

'Where on earth did that come from?' She looked quite amazed.

'Oh, it's just that the true nature of time is one of the

things Zak and I discussed.'

'I should have guessed,' she laughed. 'But don't let me interrupt you, please continue.'

'Well, according to him the idea of time as a continuum that flows *from* the past, *through* the present and *into* the future is just a human construct that allows our relatively limited brains to make sense of this reality we're experiencing. Whereas in fact time is really just a series of discrete *now-moments*.'

'Absolutely,' enthused Chloe. 'All the modern self-help books tell us that *now* is the only thing that truly exists... which is exactly why we can create our reality *afresh* in each new now-moment, if we ignore the supposed past and future.'

'Yes, we talked about this too.' Now I no longer had Zak it was refreshing to be able to share ideas with someone who seemed to see things the same way as I did.

'The best example is modern sports stars,' she continued. 'Some of the most successful have started to use the services of specialist psychologists. And what's the main message they emphasise?'

'To *stay in the moment*?' Although I wasn't a massive sports fan, from the odd news report and so on this had struck me too. 'For example, in tennis or golf, to forget about the *last* shot, especially if it was bad, and just reset. But at the same time not to think *ahead* to winning the match, championship or whatever, even if it's potentially only a few shots away... and instead just concentrate on *this shot now*.'

'Perfectly put. So how do you think this applies to the

idea of different lives? After all, many writers and therapists rightly emphasise the power of *now*, but then still happily go back to talking about *past* and even *future* lives.'

'When surely the two things are mutually incompatible... because if all *time* is now, then all *lives* must be happening now too?'

'Thank you... that's *exactly* the point. It seems to me that it's the product of woolly thinking. The problem, of course, is that the idea of all lives happening at the same time is incredibly difficult for us to get our heads around... especially when they involve different historical eras. Even I still don't understand the idea *logically* at all, and I've been thinking and talking about it for some time. But I do know that what *is* logical is that *if* time doesn't really exist *then* past lives can't really exist either, and a great many of us... gurus, writers, therapists et al... have been looking at it all wrong for some time.'

'Ok, I'm absolutely with you so far on the theory. But you still haven't explained why all this makes any *practical* difference.'

'Well, first I want you to tell me something. What's your understanding of the term *karma*?'

'It's where you reap what you sow and all that.'

'Yes, and in the context of the life you're living now you could argue it fits perfectly with the idea of creating your own reality. Because the attitudes and beliefs built up from your apparent past *do* typically dictate what you experience in the *present*... even if a real witch or wizard could break those karmic bonds in an instant and reshape their life completely anew.' She was smiling now. 'The problem is, of course, most of us aren't as adept as witches and wizards as we might like.'

'Amen to that,' I said. 'I'm living proof.'

'Correction, Zoe,' she chided me. 'You *were* living proof. Not any more.'

'Ok, ok, you're quite right, I'll be more careful with my words next time. I know they're important.'

'Good. Anyway, to return to the issue at hand, the practical problem arises when we start trying to apply the concept of karma to apparently past lives. If I had a pound for every time I've heard a client explain bad experiences as the result of bad karma from a past life or, worse still, insist *I'm working out all my bad karma in this life, that's why I'm suffering so much* – well, let's just say I'd be a very rich young woman.'

'Yes, I've occasionally heard similar things.'

'And *that's* where the problem lies... because as soon as people talk like that they're immediately limiting their power to create whatever life they want for themselves in *this* experience they're having in the *here and now*. Whereas I happen to think that every single one of us, whatever our colour, creed, social status and so on, is what we might call a *creator god* in our own right, with the ability to manifest whatever current reality we want for ourselves... where the sky is literally the limit.'

'Wow!' I thought about this for a moment. ''That's a pretty powerful message... they should teach *that* in schools and churches.'

'I wish. Maybe one day.'

'But what about the age-old question of people born into

poverty, or with other disadvantages... surely they don't have the same opportunities to create the life they want as those who are more fortunate?'

'Very good point Zoe... you've hit the nail on the head again. We create our lives subject only to any limitations imposed by what we might call our *birth givens*.'

'So... what sex we are, our physical and psychological strengths and weaknesses, the social and economic status of our parents... that sort of thing?'

'Exactly that. Think of it as *painting the best picture we can with the palette we've been given*.'

'But who decides on our birth givens then?'

'Perhaps they're chosen for us by our *higher self*.'

'I've come across that expression many times... but it often seems to mean something different so I get confused.'

'Well, to me it's that higher aspect of our consciousness that is truly god-like and resides in higher planes of awareness. You remember I mentioned the author Anton Wali in our first session?'

'Yes... you recommended *The Power of You* I think it was called?'

'Well, he actually uses the term *supersoul*, which pretty accurately sums up how I see it too.'

'Meaning that we each have a *soul* that survives in the afterlife, but our *supersoul* is operating at a higher level again?'

'Precisely,' she beamed.

'Ok, makes sense. But to bring it back to my situation then, I guess my most challenging birth given was being rejected by my real mum and then by my parents? Because I was so young these were things I had no control over, right?'

'Yes, spot on. It's only when we reach the point where we're tending to control our lives and making most of the decisions that creating our reality for ourselves really kicks in.'

'And presumably that happens for different people at different times... some have adulthood thrust on them very early, while others are much later developers.'

'Spot on again.'

I paused to think. 'So when people are born into vastly different circumstances it's not just a lottery, or God working in mysterious ways, or a reward or punishment for past karma. It's actually our higher selves trying out different combinations?'

'Bravo Zoe, bravo. Not only that but our higher selves or supersouls project multiple aspects of themselves into what we perceive as different historical time periods... although as we've said in reality all these lives are playing out alongside each other in the *eternal now*.'

'Oh my... now we *are* pushing the boundaries.' I paused again to think. 'But if all lives are playing out concurrently, how come in my first three sets of dreams I saw the subject dying? Doesn't that mean their lives were over and done with and couldn't be changed?'

'That's a great question, and not an easy one to answer. How would it sound if I suggested that what you saw in each set of dreams was the most likely scenario for that person's life at that particular now-moment, given all the decisions they'd made up to that point, their underlying beliefs and so on. The same will be true of each one of us. We each have a *most likely* future already mapped out.'

Again I couldn't help but take the next logical step. 'But, of course, if I massively change my thinking, beliefs and decision-making at any point I then massively alter that most likely future.'

This time Chloe didn't even say anything, she just beamed and gave me a double thumbs up. My confidence growing and as inquisitive as ever, I wanted to really push the conversation on. 'So, if we're going this far, we may as well tackle the big question... *why* are our higher selves doing all this?'

'Ah... yes, that *is* the big question, isn't it? The best answer I've come across is that they project aspects of themselves not just into different time periods in this reality, but also into all sorts of other realities or universes, operating at all sorts of frequencies or vibratory levels, most of which are probably very different from this one. In fact some people suggest these can be likened to various computer games that our higher selves invent to play in, and that we just happen to be focused on the one called *human life on planet earth*... although there may even be multiple versions just of this game.'

'Wow... that *is* properly mind-boggling. Yet now I think about it Zak did talk about some scientists suggesting that, contrary to appearances, all universes or realities are indeed virtual or digital.'

'Which is actually my favoured way of looking at it, because then everything ties together perfectly. But you don't have to go this far for everything else we've discussed to still make sense.'

'Ok, sure.' I paused again. 'But that still doesn't explain what's the *point* of all these games?'

'According to some the answer lies in understanding that *consciousness itself* underlies and creates everything... and our higher selves, and us as individual aspects thereof, are just particular expressions of a more universal consciousness that probably expresses itself in ways we couldn't even imagine.'

'Ok, yes... but you know what I'm going to ask next. *Why* does it want to express itself at all? What's the point?'

'Perhaps all consciousness ever wants to do is know itself better by adding to its databanks of *experience*.'

For once in this conversation I was lost for words. These were huge, huge concepts that I'd need time to digest. But my initial reaction was one of resonance. The ideas somehow *felt* right.

Chloe broke into my reverie. 'I wouldn't normally let a session develop in this way, but I know you're keen to understand the broader context of any therapy we do together... and I do believe it's helpful for those who are interested... although not all my clients want to go this far, naturally. It's also fascinating when I encounter someone like you who, having come across some of these ideas before, seems to naturally resonate with my own broader perspective. But now I think we should return to our therapeutic objective, don't you?'

'Absolutely,' I replied. 'And the one thing I still don't understand is who the protagonists in my various dreams were. Even if they weren't past lives, surely they must be connected to me somehow in order for me to have identified with them so strongly?'

'Ok, again I like Wali's explanation. He suggests they're *resonant souls* who are *you* in as much as they're other projections or aspects of *your* higher self or supersoul. And the reason they're resonant is they're facing similar challenges to you... in this case, as you know, rejection.'

'Yes, that makes perfect sense... and it wasn't just rejection, was it? The last two dream-lives included challenges relating to having young children, even if they were in a very different context?'

'Well spotted.'

'So actually what we're saying is that, rather than me inheriting some sort of *bad karma* from these resonant souls, in fact if I manage to overcome my challenges with rejection in this life, that might somehow bleed through to them and make their lives better?'

'I would say so, yes... as long as they're open to your positive influence. The trick would be for each of you to pick up on the positive influences from the others wherever and however you can – be it in dreams, sudden flashes of inspiration and intuition, or whatever – but to blank out the negative or unhelpful ones.'

'I'm not sure there's much in the way of positives I can take from their lives though?'

'Maybe there isn't. Maybe *you're* the one who's really going to crack this rejection thing,' she suggested, smiling.

'Like a full-blown superhero,' I grinned back. 'In any case, that's as maybe, but it still begs the question of why I had the dreams in the first place?'

'Again that's not so easy to answer. But what I *would* say

is that our higher selves can be very creative in trying to get us to wake up to the fact that we're much more than just our so-called *physical*, human selves.'

'So as much as anything else this was one way to get me thinking about who or what I really am?'

'That would be my best guess.'

'But wait... so the original messages in the mirror... they were from my higher self too?'

'Sounds like it, doesn't it?'

'But how would that work? Who actually *wrote* them?'

'Who can say? But would it be beyond the bounds of possibility for your higher self to have put you into a trance state in which you wrote them but didn't remember anything about it?'

'Oh wow... I'd never thought of it like that, that's kind of creepy. But I guess not, no. And there was me blaming my sister!' I laughed and shook my head as I collected my thoughts.

'So let's see if I've got this right. Forgetting the theory, the important practical point is that if I'd *believed* those were my own past lives, and that their bad karma carried over into this life, then that *could* have negatively impacted my life now – just like any other deeply held belief. Whereas at the end of the day the important thing is to concentrate on making the life I'm experiencing now the best it can be... and that in turn means overcoming any blockages that are preventing me from creating the reality of my dreams.'

Chloe leant back in her chair, a look of deep contentment on her face. 'And with that, my dear Zoe, our work here is done.'

twenty three

Even while I was having therapy I was thinking about how to really *seal the deal*, and I knew it meant a trip back to my childhood home. I needed to confront my parents, and especially to talk to mother without father interfering, so I phoned her to arrange a convenient time. She was keen to know why I wanted to visit for the first time in years, but I was suitably vague.

When I arrived on a bitterly cold afternoon in early February, after a lengthy journey on busses and trains, she seemed pleased to see me even if a little anxious. But as always there was no hug. We exchanged a few awkward pleasantries over a cup of tea in the kitchen, and I told her I hadn't been too well and had had some therapy. But she didn't seem to react much so I just came out with it.

'Mum... look, this is awkward, but there's something I need to ask you about.' She knew what was coming and stepped straight in, her voice suddenly clipped and harsh.

'I don't know where she is. I've never heard from her since the day she left you with us. I don't even know if she's still alive.'

That was a real blow, but I recovered myself. 'What about my real father?'

'Now *he* was a very nice boy, very bright.' She seemed to soften as she spoke of him. 'I only met him the once but I could tell he loved her with all his heart.'

'So what went wrong?' I guess I was still looking for some

sort of fairy tale.

'The usual story. We came from a pretty good home... our father was a doctor in the West End, you know?'

'I've never heard you talk about my grandparents before.'

'Yes, well... there's a reason. They were none too happy when I fell for your father... said he wasn't the right *class*. But he was a *real* man... a loveable rogue I used to call him. They told me to choose between him and them, and I chose love.'

'And my mum?'

'She got in with the wrong crowd, with all the drugs and nonsense, so they pretty much disowned her too. She was a real livewire, my sister.' She said this with a tinge of sadness, almost as if she missed her. 'Anyway she cleaned up for a while after she met your dad. But then, after you were born, she got depressed and took up with them again. People didn't even talk about post-natal depression in those days, you were just supposed to get on with it and soldier on.'

'Poor mum. It must have been so hard.' Hearing about her like this for the first time was very emotional for me.

'I suppose it was. Anyway this time she got onto the hard stuff, and that was the beginning of the end. Your dad stuck with her for about a year, he really tried to help her, but in the end he couldn't stand it any more so he left. No one could blame him... in those days a man couldn't take on a child alone while the mother was still around, even if he wanted to. So she got worse and worse until she just couldn't copy any more... and that's when she handed you over to us.'

'So...' I was fighting back tears now, 'so, I guess she blamed me for what happened to her?'

'*Blamed* you?' She looked incredulous. 'Oh my good lord no. She *loved* you with all her heart.'

So *that* was the explanation for my fleeting image of her looking so incredibly sad – it must have been when she knew she had to give me away. And now the dam broke. Over the years I'd learned how to cry, I'd learned how to *really* cry, but this was different. This time, at last, they were tears of sorrow, yes, but mixed with unadulterated joy. *She did love me! I wasn't rejected! I was loved! My real mum loved me so much she knew she had to give me away to protect me!*

It was some time before I was calm enough to say anything and, for the first time ever, mother put her arms round me and cried too. It was almost as if a dam inside her had burst too, and all the guilt she felt over how I'd been treated as a child was now flooding out.

'I'm so sorry Zoe... I'm so, so sorry. I didn't know what else to do. I saw the man I loved change so much after you arrived that I found it hard not to blame you too... even though I knew deep down it was wrong.'

For the first time ever we looked properly into each other's eyes. 'It's ok mum,' I said through the tears. 'It's ok. I understand.'

'Can you ever... can you ever forgive me?' She looked so pitiful.

'Of course I can mum. But I need to talk to father too. My healing won't be complete until I do.'

'I know love,' she smiled weakly. 'I always expected this would happen one day. I don't know how it will go, but I understand why you need to do it. Anyway, he'll be home any minute.'

And he was. He walked through the door and saw us sat close together, holding each others' hands. Although she'd warned him I was coming, he clearly hadn't expected this. 'Bugger me, look what the bleedin' cat's dragged in. What do *you* want? Come to scrounge money of us now you've run out, I s'pose?' He'd obviously heard about me moving out of the cottage from Kim, who I'd finally spoken to not long before. In any case, his reaction to seeing me was no surprise.

'Nice to see you too father. At least you're always consistent.'

'Don't you come the 'igh and mighty with me young lady. I can still put you across me bleedin' knee.'

He looked his normal aggressive self as mother tried to calm him. 'Don't love, please. She's come to *talk* to us.'

'You keep out of it. This is between me an' 'er. If it's a bleedin' talkin' to she wants, I'll 'appily oblige.'

'No, I don't want to be talked *to*. I want *you* to *listen* for once. Sit down and keep quiet!' Even I was surprised by my authoritative tone and, taken aback, he did exactly as he was told.

'If you thought I was still the compliant, timid little girl you turned me into all those years ago... I've got news for you. I've changed.' He was still unsettled, eyes wide, mouth slightly ajar. Sad as it was to see, maybe he *was* just the typical bully who folded when finally confronted.

'I know all about the promise you made to yourself. I know when I arrived it really upset your plans, and you struggled with money in a way you never wanted to again. I get all that, and I sympathise. But…' Standing now I stared straight down into his eyes too. I saw only fear. Again I was surprised at just how firm my voice was – louder than usual, but falling short of shouting. I was in control at last.

'But you had no right! For pity's sake man, I was just an innocent little girl! It wasn't my fault! You didn't have one scrap of pity for me… and you bullied mum and Kim so they turned against me too! For all those years I had no one to turn to. No one!'

I paused to let my message sink in before drawing close to his ear, quieter this time. 'You should be completely ashamed of yourself. I do believe in forgiveness, but not for *you*, though I hold no grudge… simply because, to me, *you no longer even exist*.'

He sat staring straight ahead, tears forming in the corners of his eyes. I kissed mother on the cheek and stepped out into the cold air.

Walking briskly away, I held my head higher than ever before.

twenty four

So that was how I finally got well. Properly well I mean. I'd finally learned that the heavy burdens I'd been carrying around had acted as subconscious blockages that prevented me from making my conscious desires about love and work and so on come true. But now the sky really was the limit. Especially with the lifting of the cloud the pills had produced I sensed a level of creativity simmering under the surface that was way stronger than anything before – a creativity that could now be unleashed in all its glory.

I went for dinner with Johnny and Marjorie towards the end of February. I'd deliberately suspended our weekly get-togethers while seeing Chloe so as not to have to talk about our work, while she'd had to maintain client confidentiality so had simply told them it was *going well*. But naturally they were keen to know more, and Johnny was – well, just Johnny.

'Come on then, don't keep us in suspense... how the devil did it go? Did she *fix* you?'

'Johnny Fawcett, you really are the most rude, inconsiderate, insensitive man I think I've ever come across!' For once Marjorie was being serious and gave him a look that Medusa would've struggled to match. I suspect she may have warned him not to be too direct with me, but he'd just ignored her and was now paying the price.

'Sorry ma dear,' he muttered into his chin, casting a suitably sheepish sidelong glance in my direction, his face now even redder than usual.

'I should think so too,' Marjorie continued, but I held up my hand.

'Please, it's ok. I know you only asked because you care.' Johnny dared to lift his head a little.

'Well, he should know better than to pry like that at his age.' She shot him another look and, as his head lowered once more, steered the conversation in a more general direction. 'So how are you coping in that horrid little room?'

'Actually fine... amazing in fact!' Johnny looked up and they were both equally surprised. 'I know... it sounds crazy... but I've found that now I'm feeling more positive I can just blank out the noise. I'm completely off the pills and I've even started writing again!'

'You must be tougher than you look to blank out noise like that.' Johnny glanced at his wife to check if he was ok to speak again and, emboldened, continued: 'If it was me I'd shoot the blighters!'

'Well it isn't you so just keep your nose out of it.' He was in trouble again, but less this time. 'Zoe has got enough problems with her neighbours without you inflaming the situation. If the police and courts were to get involved they'd probably wrap them around their little fingers, and *you'd* be the one who ended up in jail. Mind you, the way you behave sometimes, maybe that's the best place for you.' She couldn't help breaking into a small smile. It was clear she could never be angry with the man she loved for very long.

'Well, as I said, amazingly it's really not a problem for me any more.'

'But I thought authors need a proper environment where they can get *in the zone*. I believe that's the modern expression?' asked Marjorie.

'That's what they all *say*, and they complain that if they don't have the right surroundings they get *writer's block* and their *muse* doesn't speak to them and all that. But do you know what? I think if you're really focused, and really motivated, it doesn't matter where you are or what's going on around you. You just shut it out and let it flow.' I was surprised at how I was opening up and expressing thoughts I hadn't even shared with myself before now.

'That's the spirit,' smiled Johnny. 'Bit of the old stiff upper lip never did anyone any harm. Most of these writer blighters wouldn't know what hit them in the army. Discipline, that's what they need.'

'Well to be fair from what I've read some writers are actually very disciplined. But anyway it feels great now that everything is just flowing much more than before.'

'Why that's wonderful Zoe!' Marjorie didn't do flattery or condescension – she was genuinely delighted for me.

'It is. I don't want to bore you… but perhaps I can describe how it feels? I don't have anyone else to talk to about this.' I was bursting to share what had been happening.

'Of course!' they chimed together.

'Well it's strange. I've never felt it before, but this time I get the sense that somehow the book has already been written quite perfectly on some other level.' They glanced at each other, clearly intrigued. 'It's as if it already exists… and all I have to do now is have as clear a head as possible and sort of *channel* it through the keyboard.'

'You mean it's coming from... what... a higher dimension sort of job?' I knew that Marjorie had talked to Chloe about her spiritual views and had some sympathy for them, but I didn't expect this from Johnny. He saw my startled look and grinned. 'Oh, I'm not quite as straight-laced as I look you know. When you've seen some of the things I've seen, you learn *there's more things in heaven and earth*... and all that.'

'Don't let that bluff exterior fool you Zoe... he's full of surprises. There's even a heart beating in their somewhere.' They winked at each other. Clearly Johnny's interjection had come as no surprise to his wife.

'Well... yes... a higher dimension, that's exactly what I mean. One clue is that I'm particularly productive when I wake up in the morning, or following my afternoon siesta. If you really want to know my best guess is that my higher self, or some other entity from the spirit world, is prepping me while I sleep.'

So it turned out I *could* talk to others about some of this stuff, and they wouldn't *necessarily* consign me to the madhouse. Perhaps people generally were far more open-minded than I'd previously assumed? I made a mental note: *stop judging and making assumptions when it comes to matters of the spirit.*

As soon as I'd achieved the final release of visiting my parents I worked day and night in my room, oblivious to all distractions. Apart from recommencing my weekly suppers with Johnny and Marjorie, my only relaxation was to walk or run in the surrounding countryside – which I tried to do most days to keep some sort of balance. Having said that it turned out that surrounding myself with mother nature acted as an additional boost to creativity, and ideas seemed to just flow through me, especially if I'd been at all stuck on something.

By the end of April, just three months after finishing therapy, I had the rough first draft of a book I finally knew was worth reading.

Now there was just one more piece of the jigsaw.

Zak could tell straight away I was different.

Imagine my huge relief when he told me he'd always believed I'd get myself well somehow – even though he also revealed that for a long time he'd felt he might have to leave me for that to happen. I was just incredibly thankful that he'd waited. I moved into his house almost immediately after we first saw each other again. As for the cottage, for the time being I'd keep it on, still rented out, but it was time for us to be together properly.

Naturally we discussed my therapy too. 'So are you suggesting that everyone has to have regression therapy to be happy and successful? I mean, I don't want to sound arrogant, but I honestly don't feel I need it.'

'No, no, not at all sweetheart. You probably don't. You tend to think positively anyway, and seem to have had little problem with creating the life you want. It's just that some of us face more challenges than others, and sometimes we need help with them. It doesn't make any of us better or worse or anything, we're all just different.'

I proceeded to recap the entire conversation I'd had with

Chloe about how my subconscious had been programmed by my real mum's thoughts about children; about the idea of parallel lives despite the appearance of different human eras, and my dream protagonists being resonant souls facing similar challenges with rejection; about the need to concentrate on painting the best picture we can in this life now, rather than fixating on supposed past-life karma, the will of fickle gods, or blind chance and so on; about our higher selves or supersouls choosing our birth givens to experiment with different combinations; and about these higher aspects of consciousness creating multiple universes or realities to act as digital playgrounds, all so they can add to their databanks of experience.

'That's really fascinating, and makes a lot of sense,' said Zak eventually, looking thoughtful. 'I'll need time to take it all on board, but something tells me these ideas will be important in my own work too.'

'That would be great... all these things need to be pulled together so people like you can break through and change the paradigm. *Materialism has had its day!*' I was surprised at my sudden passion, but Zak loved it.

'Amen to that my sweet!' He took me in his arms and swung me around. 'And what with my lack of challenges and imperfections I must be an *ascended master* or some such... so it should be pretty easy for me.'

Of course he was joking, but something told me to sound a note of caution. 'Well, don't count your chickens just yet *master*. Despite us creating our own experience the vast majority of the time, I've got a feeling that challenges can occasionally come out of nowhere to bite us in the bum...

perhaps when we least expect them.'

We set a date for September. We wanted some time to plan our wedding, but after nine months apart we didn't want to delay either. My parents were invited and, while it was a relief that as expected father refused point-blank, for once in her life mother stood up to him and came along with Kim, Gerry and Alice. As well as Johnny, Marjorie, Chloe and Greg I invited a select few old friends, as did Zak, but there were only about thirty of us in all. We wanted it that way. Neither of us went in for big public displays.

Although we weren't religious per se I wanted to get married in the church in front of the cottage, and my beloved didn't object. I wore a simple, sleeveless, full-length satin dress – veils and trains weren't my style – while as maids of honour Kim and little Alice had similar ones in pale green. Zak and his best man Josh, an old school friend I'd met only briefly when he came down one weekend, looked so handsome in their morning suits and top hats. Of course the reception was held in the hotel restaurant. We hadn't been there since my thirtieth, but this would more than erase the painful memories of that night.

We had the most wonderful afternoon imaginable. The service went perfectly, the food afterwards was delicious, everyone was getting on, and Josh's speech was hilarious – stopping just short of being embarrassing. When Zak stood up I think I was happier than I'd ever been when he introduced me as 'Mrs Sheridan… although she insists she's still going to write under her maiden name'. He was charming, witty and loving in equal measure – but was also building up to two announcements we'd agreed upon beforehand.

'As if this day isn't momentous enough already, we've some further news for you.' He could control an audience brilliantly and, even though there'd been plenty of heckles earlier, a hushed, expectant silence now descended.

'First of all, you all know about Zoe's incredible perseverance with her writing, even when the rest of us... me included sometimes, to my eternal shame... doubted her.' He glanced down with sadness in his eyes, even though he knew I'd forgiven him. 'Well, that perseverance has been rewarded. Last week she signed a contract with one of the UK's largest publishers for her latest book!' There was great cheering and applause, even from such a relatively small group. 'And it will be published next March for those of you who want to order an advance copy!' Cue laughter. He waited for it to die down, so he had their full attention again. 'But that's not all... not by any stretch. They've also told her they're going to submit it for next year's prestigious Orange Prize for women's fiction!' There was a short stunned silence before the cheering and applause started up again.

'There's more, there's more!' Quietening them with outstretched arms, again he waited for the hubbub to subside. 'It's only my small contribution... and I'm sorry I kept this one quiet darling.' He turned to look at me again, smiling gently, before continuing. 'But also last week I found out I've been very fortunate, and that the BBC want me to front a new documentary series about my work.' The room erupted again and I jumped up to hug him.

'Why on earth didn't you tell me? That's so fantastic!' I shouted in his ear.

'It's no big deal, Mrs. Sheridan.'

'It most certainly is! Oh, we're both going to be taken seriously, and we'll be in demand and... life just doesn't get better, does it?'

'No, Zo, it really doesn't.' He kissed me tenderly as everyone cheered until, after longer than was probably decent, we reluctantly drew apart. 'Shall we tell them the other news now?' he asked, loud enough that everyone could hear despite the excited chatter.

'I suppose you'd better,' I laughed, our arms still wrapped around each other.

'Ladies and gentlemen.' He calmed them once more. 'There is one final piece of news to report. Last night my wife...' again he turned and smiled at me proudly, 'made me even happier than when she agreed to take me as her husband. She informed me that she's expecting our first child.'

We beamed as everyone stood up and clapped and cheered even more. That exact moment really is one of my most treasured memories.

In November I went for my first scan, and the natural tension all prospective parents face dissipated as soon as we found out I was carrying a healthy baby boy. We decided to call him Michael, after Zak's father. We were equally over the moon when, in early March of the following year, we heard my book had been longlisted for the Orange – which meant it now had a one-in-twenty chance of winning.

The tension built as the judges beavered away until, five weeks later, the six shortlisted books were announced – and I was on it! The joy of this wonderful news was almost unparalleled, because just getting this far would garner plenty of sales and publicity. Now we just had to wait for the awards ceremony in late May to find out if I'd been able to go all the way. I called Kim, who was ecstatic as you'd expect, but mother was pretty much back to her usual self. I guess exposure to father had desensitised her again – and to be honest I really, really didn't care any more.

That night, as I lay in bed next to Zak – we couldn't cuddle for long because of my bulge, so we just held hands – at last I had some definitive answers to the questions my higher self had posed all those years before.

Who are you? A spiritual being on an experiential human path, painting the best picture I could with the palette I'd been given – and, yes, no shame in saying it, doing a pretty darned good job too.

Are you happy? Yes, yes, yes! I had my wonderful husband, our imminent baby, our friends, my sister and her family, my shortlisted book, Zak's television series, our beautiful houses, and so on – how could I be anything other than supremely grateful, even while forced to acknowledge that I myself had actually manifested pretty much all of it. But, most important of all, I was happy *inside*. The people and possessions *outside* you can come and go, and they do. That's one of the big tests we face – we have to learn to love with all our hearts, yet not be *too* attached to or dependant on anyone or anything – and we can only achieve this if we're truly content with who and what we are.

And that answered my third question: *Who do you love?* Yes I loved Zak, and now it was with *all* my heart, unlike before. But now I loved someone else even more. I loved me. Truly, madly, deeply. That more than anything was the key.

Finally I'd learned how to create the life I really wanted because I'd risen to the challenge of rejection in my childhood and waved goodbye to all the Doubting Thomas's in my subconscious.

I truly had learned how to live.

twenty five

'The winner is...' repeats the woman at the lectern, quieter now, tears filling her eyes. 'It's Zoe... Zoe Smith.'

Even though many of these people are ostensibly my rivals for the prize, the whole place erupts with delight, many of them standing and clapping and cheering. I feel a huge release. *I've done it! I'VE DONE IT!!* Everything I've dreamt about has finally come true.

Zak has passed baby Michael over to Kim and is slowly making his way forward through the throng, looking more nervous than I've ever seen him. It's not as if he's not used to public speaking. But, then again, these are exceptional circumstances.

He's reached the lectern now.

Of course I'm thrilled and excited, but there's a tinge of sadness too.

It's only natural.

Anyway I'm going to be quiet. I want to hear what he's going to say.

'Ladies and gentlemen, I'm sure you understand this is not an easy speech to give. If only Zoe herself was here to make it.' He pauses as he fights admirably to control himself. 'But I know she would be *so* proud that her work has at last been recognised, after all her struggles and heartache.'

Applause ripples round the room.

'She would especially want me to thank Isabelle, her agent, who finally got her the breakthrough she so richly deserved, as well as Elizabeth her editor and everyone else involved in this great publishing effort, for believing in her and doing such a great job. She would also want me to congratulate and commiserate with the other authors, whose work she very much admired. And she would of course want me to thank, indeed pay tribute to, the judging panel... for their wonderful taste and good sense.'

He pauses until the polite laughter dies down.

'Above all, though, I would like to propose a toast to the woman I love. I miss her more than I can say. And to our little baby boy Michael, who will always remind me of her.'

He begins to break down, but pulls himself together again with a huge effort of will.

'Ladies and gentlemen, please raise your glasses.'

The members of the audience rise to their feet once more and happily follow the instruction.

'To Zoe. Godspeed my darling. You didn't believe that leaving this life is the end of the journey, and I'm sure you're soaring high, wherever you are.'

With that he turns his head away, weeping gently.

'To Zoe!' echoes around the room, and for a moment there is silence... until again the applause begins.

postscript

Sorry to spring the news of my passing on you like that, but it was all so sudden. By the way, the chair of the judging panel was at pains to point out that they'd already come to a pretty-much unanimous decision just beforehand. I don't want you thinking I only won with a sympathy vote.

Anyway, I know death during childbirth is incredibly rare in the developed world these days, but it turns out I had an undiagnosed heart condition and it just couldn't take the strain. As for who decided on my early death – who knows? Maybe having overcome my challenges I'd kind of *passed the test* and there was no need for me to hang around, as pleasurable as it would have been. Maybe also some higher aspect of Zak wanted to set him a new challenge – one not of his own making.

Of course there's a big part of me that's hugely sad to leave him, and my beautiful baby as well. But already what you might call my *soul perspective* seems to be taking over, and I've a strong sense they'll meet this test with dignity and love. Zak knows that to give in to his gut-wrenching grief – as understandable as it would be – would only keep me energetically bound to him and prevent me from properly moving on. So he's already attempting to let me go with love, grace and gratitude for my part in his life. It's supremely hard, but he's rising to the challenge beautifully.

Talking of which, I *had* better be getting along. I've seen everything I want to see, including mother and father at my funeral – *both* crying their eyes out, would you believe? A bright light has been just on the edge of my awareness for a while now, and I know it's waiting to draw me in.

Not only is this clearly a whole new beginning rather than an ending, but I seem to have some sort of *innate knowing* that it's one with limitless possibilities. To say I'm excited about what lies ahead hardly does justice to my sense of eager anticipation.

But before I go I'm sure there's something else.

Oh… yes! I guess you want to know what my book was about? Well, in a nutshell, the hero is a struggling author who perseveres against all the odds.

the Supersoul Series

all published by Rational Spirituality Press
see *www.rspress.org* and *www.ianlawton.com*

RESEARCH BOOKS

[Volume 1] SUPERSOUL (2013) is the main reference book for Supersoul Spirituality, containing out-of-body and channelled evidence that each and every one of us is a holographic reflection of a supersoul that has power way beyond our wildest imaginings.

[Volume 2] THE POWER OF YOU (2014) compares modern channelled wisdom from a variety of well-known sources, all emphasising that each of us is consciously or unconsciously creating every aspect of our own reality, and that this is what the current consciousness shift is all about.

[Volume 3] AFTERLIFE (2019) is a state-of-the-art, clear, reliable guide to the afterlife based on the underlying consistencies in traditional channelled material and modern out-of-body research.

SIMPLE BOOKS

SH*T DOESN'T JUST HAPPEN!! (2016) introduces Supersoul Spirituality by explaining how and why we ourselves create or attract everything we experience in our adult lives... so that we are never victims of chance, God's will, our karma or our life plans.

WHAT JESUS WAS REALLY SAYING (2016) is a fundamental reinterpretation of the Christian message that uses excerpts from the Gospels to propose that, through his supposed miracles, Jesus was trying to show us that each of us is a creator god of the highest order and can manipulate the illusion we call reality at will.

THE GOD WHO SOMETIMES SCREWED UP (2018) charts the author's progression from motorcycle and car racer, to pyramid explorer and researcher of ancient civilisations, to spiritual philosopher… with analysis and examples of how he has created or manifested all the various aspects of his life, both good and bad.

DEATH IS AN ADVENTURE!! (2019) is a simple yet essential guide to the afterlife, which answers all your questions such as why you will continue to exist, what to expect and how best to prepare. Based on evidence not belief, it describes the unlimited possibilities we have to create wondrous new experiences… as long as we have a reliable map of the territory.

IAN LAWTON was born in 1959. Formerly an accountant, sales exec, business and IT consultant and avid bike and car racer, in his mid-thirties he changed tack completely to become a writer-researcher specialising in ancient history and, more recently, spiritual philosophy. His first two books, *Giza: The Truth* and *Genesis Unveiled,* sold over 30,000 copies worldwide.

In his non-fiction *Books of the Soul Series* he originated the ideas of Rational Spirituality and of the holographic soul. But since 2013 he has been developing the more radical worldview of Supersoul Spirituality in the *Supersoul Series*. A short film clip discussing the latter can be found at *www.ianlawton.com* and on YouTube. This is his first novel.

Lightning Source UK Ltd.
Milton Keynes UK
UKHW052304050922
408358UK00014B/1256

9 781739 144500